Nora Roberts is the *New York Times* bestselling author of more than two hundred novels. A born storyteller, she creates a blend of warmth, humour and poignancy that speaks directly to her readers and has earned her almost every award for excellence in her field. The youngest of five children, Nora Roberts lives in western Maryland. She has two sons.

Visit her website at www.noraroberts.com

Also available by Nora Roberts

Nora Roberts

Times Change

MILLS & BOON

This edition published in Great Britain 2016
By Mills & Boon, an imprint of HarperCollins*Publishers*
1 London Bridge Street, London, SE1 9GF

Times Change © 1989 Nora Roberts

ISBN: 978-0-263-92368-1

29-1216

Our policy is to use papers that are natural, renewable and recyclable products and made from wood grown in sustainable forests. The logging and manufacturing processes conform to the legal environmental regulations of the country of origin.

Printed and bound
by CPI Group (UK) Ltd, Croydon, CR0 4YY

For Isabel, who's always been ahead of her time

Chapter 1

He knew the risks. He was a man who was willing to take them. One misstep, one bad call, and it would all be over, essentially before it had begun. But he had always considered life a gamble. Often—perhaps too often—he had allowed his impulses to rule and plunged recklessly into potentially dangerous situations. In this case, he had figured the odds painstakingly.

Two years of his life had been spent calculating, simulating, constructing. The most minute details had been considered, computed and analyzed. He was a very patient man—when it came to his work. He knew what *could* happen. Now it was time to discover what would.

More than a few of his associates believed he had crossed the line between genius and madness. Even those who were enthusiastic about his theories worried that he'd gone too far. Popular opinion didn't concern him. Results did. And results of this, the greatest experience of his life, would be personal. Very personal.

Seated behind the wide curve of the control panel, he looked more like a buccaneer at the helm of a ship than a scientist on the verge of discovery. But science was his life, and that made him as true an explorer as the ancient Columbus and Magellan.

He believed in chance, in the purest sense of the word—the unpredictable possibility of existence.

He was here now to prove it. In addition to his calculations, the technology at his command, his knowledge and his computations, he needed one element that any explorer required for success.

Luck.

He was alone now in the vast, silent sea of space, beyond the traffic patterns, beyond the last charted quadrant. There was an intimacy here between man and his dreams that could never be achieved in a laboratory. For the first time since his voyage had begun, he smiled. He had been in his laboratory too long.

The solitude was soothing, even tempting. He'd almost forgotten what it was like to be truly alone, with only his own thoughts for company. If he'd chosen, he could have cruised along, easing back on the throttle and taking the aloneness to heart for as long as it suited him.

Up here, at the edge of man's domain, with his own planet a bright ball shrinking in the distance, he had time. And time was the key.

Resisting temptation, he logged his coordinates—speed, trajectory, distance—all meticulously calculated. His long, agile fingers moved over dials and switches. The control panel glowed green, casting a mystic aura over his sharp-featured face.

It was concentration rather than fear that narrowed his eyes and firmed his lips as he hurtled toward the sun. He knew exactly what the results would be if his calculations were off by even the slightest margin. The bright star's gravity would suck him in. It would take only a heartbeat for his ship and its occupant to be vaporized.

The ultimate failure, he thought as he stared at the luminous star that filled his viewing screen. Or the ultimate achievement. It was a gorgeous sight, this glowing, swirling light that filled the cabin and dazzled his eyes. Even at this distance, the sun held the power of life and death. Like a hot, hungry woman, it bewitched.

Deliberately he lowered the shield on the viewing screen. He pushed for more speed, watching the dials as he neared the maximum the ship could handle. A check of gauges showed him that the outside temperature was rising dramatically. He waited, knowing that beyond the protective screen the intensity of light would have seared his corneas. A man shooting toward the sun risked blindness and destruction—risked never achieving his destiny.

He waited while the first warning bell sounded, waited as the ship bucked and danced under the demands of velocity and gravity. The calm voice of the computer droned on, giving him speed, position and, most important, time.

Though he could hear his own blood pounding in his ears, his hand was steady as it urged more speed from the laboring engines.

He streaked toward the sun, faster than any man had ever been known to fly. Jaw clenched, he shoved a lever home. His ship shuddered, rocked, then tilted. End over end it tumbled—once, twice, a third time—before he could right it. His fingers gripped the controls as the force slapped him back in the chair. The cabin exploded with sound and light as he fought to hold his course.

For an instant his vision grayed and he thought fatalistically that instead of being burned up in the sun's heat he would simply be crushed by her gravity. Then his ship sprang free, like an arrow from a bow. Fighting for breath, he adjusted the controls and hurtled toward his fate.

What impressed Jacob most about the Northwest was the space. As far as he could see in any direction, there was rock and wood and sky. It was quiet, not silent but quiet, with small animals rustling in the underbrush and birds calling as they wheeled overhead. Tracks dimpling the blanket of snow around his ship told him that larger animals roamed here. More importantly, the snow itself told him that his calculations were off by at least a matter of months.

For the moment, he had to be satisfied with being approximately where he wanted to be. And with being alive.

Always meticulous, he returned to his ship to record the facts and his impressions. He had seen pictures and videos of this place and time. For the past year he had studied every scrap of information he could find on the late twentieth century. Clothes, language, sociopolitical atmosphere. As a scientist he'd been fascinated. As a man he'd been appalled and amused by turns. And baffled when he'd remembered that his brother had chosen to live here, in this primitive time and place. Because of a woman.

Jacob opened a compartment and took out a picture. An example of twentieth-century technology, he mused, as he turned the Polaroid snapshot over in his hand. He studied his brother first. Caleb's easy grin was in place. And he looked comfortable sitting on the steps of a small wooden structure, dressed in baggy jeans and a sweater. He had his arm around a woman. The woman called Libby, Jacob thought now. She was unquestionably attractive, as females went. Not as flashy as Cal's usual type, but certainly inoffensive.

Just what was there about her that had made Cal give up his home, his family and his freedom?

Because he was prepared to dislike her, Jacob tossed the picture back in its compartment. He would see this Libby for himself. Judge for himself. Then he would give Cal a swift kick and take him home.

First there were some precautions to take.

Moving from the flight deck to his personal quarters, Jacob stripped off his flight suit. The denim jeans and cotton sweater that had cost him more than he cared to remember were still in their plastic holder. Excellent reproductions, he thought as he tugged the jeans over his long legs. And, to give the devil his due, extremely comfortable.

When he was dressed, he studied himself in the mirror. If he ran into any inhabitants during his stay—a brief one, he hoped—he wanted to blend in. He had neither the time nor the inclination to attempt to explain himself to a people who were most assuredly slow-witted. Nor did he want any of the media coverage that was so popular in this time.

Though he hated to admit it, the gray sweater and the blue jeans suited him. The fit was excellent, and the material was smooth against his skin. Most importantly, in them he looked like a twentieth century man.

His dark hair nearly skimmed his shoulders. It was thick, and it was always disheveled, as he paid more attention to his work than to hairstyles. Still, it was an excellent frame for his angular face. His brows were often drawn together over dark green eyes, and his mouth, usually grim when he was poring over calculations, had an unexpected and powerful charm when he relaxed enough to smile.

He wasn't smiling now. He slung his bag over his shoulder and left the ship.

Depending on the slant of the sun rather than on his watch, Jacob decided it was just past noon. The sky was miraculously empty. It was incredible to stand under the hard blue cup and see only the faint white trail of what he assumed was the vapor trail from an old continental transport. They called them planes, he remembered, watching the stream lengthen.

How patient they must be, he mused, to sit cheerfully, shoulder to shoulder with hundreds of other people, hanging in the sky for hours just to get from one coast to another or from New York to Paris.

Then again, they didn't know any better.

Switching his gaze from sky to earth, he began to walk.

It was fortunate that the sun was bright. His preparations hadn't included a coat or any heavy outerwear. The snow beneath his boots was soft, but there was just enough of a wind to make the air uncomfortable until the hike warmed his muscles.

He was a scientist by vocation, and he could lose himself for hours, even days, in equations and experiments. But it wouldn't have occurred to him to neglect his body, either—it was as well toned and as disciplined as his mind.

He used his wrist unit to give him the bearings. At least Cal's report had been fairly specific as to where his ship had gone down and where the cabin he had stayed in when he had met this Libby was situated.

Nearly three hundred years in the future, Jacob had visited the spot and had excavated the time capsule that his brother and the woman had buried.

Jacob had left home in the year 2255. He had traveled through time and through space to find his brother. And to take him home.

As he walked he saw no signs of man, or of the posh resorts that would populate this area in another century or two. There was simply space, acres of it, untrampled and untouched. The sun cast blue shadows on the snow, and the trees towered, silent giants overhead.

Despite the logic of what he had done, the months of precise calculations, the careful working of theory into fact, he found himself chilled. The enormity of what he had achieved, where he had gone, struck him. He was standing on the ground, beneath the sky, of a planet that was more foreign to him than the moon. He was filling his lungs with air. He could watch it expel in white streams. He could feel the cold on his face and his ungloved hands. He could smell the pine and taste the crisp, clear air as it blew around him.

And he had yet to be born.

Had it been the same for his brother? No, Jacob thought, there would have been no elation, not at first. Cal had been lost, injured, confused. He hadn't set out to come here, but had been a victim of fate and circumstance. Then, vulnerable and alone, he had been bewitched by a woman. Expression grim, Jacob continued to hike.

Pausing at the stream, he remembered. A little more than two years ago—and centuries in the future—he had stood here. It had been high summer, and though the stream had changed its course over time this spot had been very much the same.

There had been grass rather than snow under his feet. But the grass would grow again, year after year, summer after summer. He had proof of that. He *was* proof of that. The stream would run fast, where now it forced its way over rock and thick islands of ice.

A little dazed, he crouched down and took a handful of snow in his ungloved hand.

He had been alone then, too, though there had been the steady drone of air traffic overhead and a huddle of mountain hotels only a few kilometers to the east. When he had uncovered the box his brother had buried he had sat on the grass and wondered.

And now he stood and wondered. If he dug for it, he would come upon the same box. The box that he had left with his parents only days before. The box would exist here, beneath his feet, just as it existed in his own time. As he existed.

If he dug it up now and carried it back to his ship, it would not be there for him to find on that high summer day in the twenty-third century. And if that was true, how could he be here, in this time, to dig it up at all?

An interesting puzzle, Jacob mused. He left it to stew in his brain as he walked.

He saw the cabin and was fascinated. No matter how many pictures, how many films or simulations he had seen, this was real. There were patches of snow melting slowly on the roof. The wood was still dark, aged by mere decades. On the glass of the windows, sunlight sparkled as it streamed through the high trees. Smoke—he could see it, as well as smell it—puffed from the stone chimney and into the hard blue sky.

Amazing, he thought, and for the first time in many hours his lips curved. He felt like a child who had discovered a unique and wonderful present under the

Christmas tree. It was his, for the moment, to explore, to analyze, to piece together and take apart until he understood it.

Shifting his bag, he walked up the snow-covered path to the steps. They creaked under his weight and turned his smile into a grin.

He didn't bother to knock. Manners were easily lost in the haze of discovery. Pushing the door open, he stepped into the cabin.

"Incredible. Absolutely incredible." His quiet voice hung in the air.

Wood, genuine and rich, gleamed around him. Stone, the kind that was chipped and dug out of the earth, merged with the wood in the form of a huge fireplace. There was a fire burning in it, crackling and hissing behind a mesh screen. The scent was wonderful. It was a small, cramped room, jammed with furniture, yet it was appealing in its cheeriness and its oddities.

Jacob could have spent hours in that room alone, examining every inch of it. But he wanted to see the rest. Muttering into his minirecorder, he started up the stairs.

Sunny yanked the wheel of the Land Rover and swore. How could she actually have believed she wanted to spend a couple of months in the cabin? Peace and quiet! Who needed it? She ground the gears as the Land Rover chugged up the hill. The idea that a few solitary weeks would give her the opportunity to sort out her life and finally decide what she wanted to do with it was ridiculous.

She knew what she wanted to do with it. Something big, something spectacular. Disgusted, she blew out a long breath that sent her blond bangs dancing. Just because she hadn't decided exactly what that something was didn't matter. She'd know it when she saw it.

Just as she always knew what it wasn't when she saw it.

It wasn't flying cargo planes—or jumping out of them. It wasn't ballet, and it wasn't touring with a rock band. It wasn't driving a truck, and it wasn't writing haiku.

Not everyone, at twenty-three, could be so specific about where her ambitions didn't lie, Sunny reminded herself as she spun the Land Rover to a halt in front of the cabin. Using the process of elimination, she should be well on her way to fame and success in another ten or twenty years.

Fingers drumming against the steering wheel, she studied the cabin. It was squat, and just homely enough not to be ugly. An old rocker stood on the porch that skirted the front. It had sat there year after year, summer and winter, for as long as she could remember. There was, she discovered, something comforting in continuity.

And yet with the comfort came a restlessness for the new, for the untouched and the unseen.

With a sigh, she sat back, ignoring the cold. What was it that she wanted that wasn't here, in this place? Or in any place she'd been? Still, when it had come time to question, when it had come time to think, she had come back here, to the cabin.

She had been born in it, had spent the first few years of her life inside it and running through the surrounding forest. Perhaps that was why she had come back when her life had seemed so pointless. Just to recapture some of that simplicity.

She loved it, really. Oh, not with the passion her sister, Libby, did. Not with the deep-rooted sentiment of their parents. But fondly, the way children often feel about an old, eccentric aunt.

Sunny couldn't imagine living there again, the way Libby and her new husband were. Day after day, night after night, without seeing another soul. Perhaps Sunny's roots were in the forest, but her heart belonged to the city, with its bright lights and its possibilities.

Just a vacation, she told herself, pulling off her woolen hat and running impatient fingers through her short hair. She was entitled to one. After all, she'd entered college at the tender age of sixteen. Too bright for her own good, her father had said more than once. After graduating just before her twentieth birthday, she had plunged into endeavor after endeavor, never finding satisfaction.

She tended to be good at whatever she did. Perhaps that was why she'd taken lessons in everything from tap dancing to tole painting. But being good at something didn't make it the right something. So she moved on, perennially restless, feeling perennially guilty for leaving things half-done.

Now it was time to settle down. So she had come here, to think, to decide, to consider. That was all. It wasn't as if she were hiding—just because she'd lost her last job. No, her last two jobs, she told herself viciously.

In any case, she had enough money to hold her for the rest of the winter—particularly since there was no place to spend any around here. If she went with her instincts and caught the next plane to Portland or Seattle—or anywhere something was happening—she'd be flat broke in a week. And she'd be damned if she'd go crawling back to her indulgent and exasperated parents.

"You said you were going to stay," she muttered as she pushed the door of the car open. "And you're going to stay until you figure out where Sunny Stone fits."

Hauling out the two bags of groceries she'd just purchased in town, she trudged through the snow. At the very least, she thought, a couple of months in the cabin would prove her self-sufficiency. If she didn't die of boredom first.

Inside, she glanced toward the fire first, satisfied that it was still burning well. Those few years in the Girl Scouts hadn't been wasted. She dumped both bags on the kitchen counter. She knew Libby would have immediately set about putting everything in its place. Sunny figured it was a waste of time to store something when you were only going to have to get it out again sooner or later.

With the same disregard, she tossed her coat over the back of a chair, then kicked her boots into a corner. Digging a candy bar out of a bag, she unwrapped it and wandered back into the living room. What she needed was a long afternoon of research. Lately she'd been toying with the idea of going back to school and trying for a law degree. The idea of arguing for a living had a certain appeal. Along with her clothes, her camera, her sketch pad, her tape recorder and her dance shoes she had packed two boxes of books on an assortment of professions.

During her first week in the cabin she had researched and discarded screenwriting as too unstable, medicine as too terrifying and running a retro clothing store as too trendy.

But law had possibilities. She could see herself as either the cold, hard-edged D.A. or the dedicated, overworked public defender.

It was worth looking into, she decided as she mounted

the stairs. And the sooner she had her focus the sooner she could get back to where there was something more exciting to do than watch the melting snow run off the gutters.

The candy bar was halfway to her mouth when she stepped into the doorway and saw him. He was standing by the bed—her bed—obviously engrossed in the fashion magazine she'd tossed on the floor the night before. It was in his hands now, and his fingers seemed to stroke the glossy paper as if it were some exotic fabric.

Though his back was to her, she could see that he was tall. He had two or three inches on her willowy five-ten. His dark hair was long enough to fall over the collar of the sweater he wore, and it looked as if he'd ridden fast in an open car. Hardly daring to breathe, she took his measure.

If he was a wayward hiker, he was dressed neatly, and sparely. The jeans showed no signs of wear. The boots he wore were unmarked, expensive and, unless she missed her guess, custom-made. No, she didn't think he was a hiker, even a foolish one who would challenge the winter mountains.

He had a lean build, though she couldn't be sure what the baggy sweater hid in the way of muscle. If he was a thief, he was a stupid one, passing the time with a magazine rather than bundling up what passed for valuables in the cabin.

Her gaze shot over to the dresser and her jewelry case. Her collection wasn't extensive, but each piece had been selected with care and a disregard for expense. And it was hers, just as the cabin was hers, just as the room he'd invaded was hers.

Furious, she dropped the candy and snatched up the closest weapon, an empty pop bottle and, brandishing it, lunged forward.

Jacob heard the movement. Out of the corner of his eye he caught a red blur. Instinct had him turning, shifting, just as the bottle whizzed by his head and smashed against the nightstand. Glass exploded with a sound like a shot.

"What the—"

Before he could utter another word, his foot was kicked out from under him and he found himself flipped neatly and sprawled on his back. He stared up at a tall, slender woman with a shiny crop of blond hair and molten gray eyes. She was crouched, arms bent, hands flexed in an ancient fighting stance.

"Don't even think about it," she warned, in a voice as smoky as her eyes. "I don't want to have to hurt you, so get up slow. Then get yourself downstairs and out. You've got thirty seconds."

Keeping his eyes on hers, he braced himself on one elbow. When dealing with a member of a primitive culture it was wise to go slowly. "Excuse me?"

"You heard me, pal. I'm a fourth-degree black belt. Mess with me and I'll crush your skull like a walnut."

She smiled when she said it. Otherwise he might have offered her excuses and explanations then and there. But she smiled, and a challenge was a challenge.

Without a word, he sprang up to land lightly on the balls of his feet in a stance that mirrored hers. He saw surprise in her eyes—not panic, surprise. He blocked her first blow, but he still felt it reverberate from his forearm to his shoulder. He shifted enough to prevent a well-aimed kick from connecting with his chin.

She was fast, he noted, fast and agile. He parried her offensive moves, staying on the defensive as he judged her. Fearless, he thought with pure admiration. A warrior in a world that still required them. And if Jacob had a weakness he would admit to, it was the love of a good fight.

He didn't toy with her. If he did, he knew, he'd end up on the floor with her foot on his throat. The kick that shot past his guard and into his rib cage was proof of that. It was an even match, he decided after five sweaty minutes, except for the fact that he had the advantage in reach and weight.

Deciding to put both to use, he feinted, blocked, then caught her in a throw that sent her flying onto the bed. Before she could recover, he spread himself over her, cautiously gripping her wrists over her head.

She was out of breath, but she wasn't out of fuel. Her eyes burning into his, she put all her strength into one last move. Just in time, he shifted his weight and avoided the knee to the groin.

"Some things never change," he muttered, and studied her while he waited for his labored breathing to slow.

She was stunning—or perhaps it was the fight that made her seem so. Her skin was flushed now, a rosy pink that enhanced the sunlight color of her hair. Its short, almost severe cut played up the elegance of her bone structure. She had sharp cheekbones. Warrior-like, he thought again. Like a Viking, or a Celt. Large, long-lidded gray eyes smoldered in frustration but not in defeat. Her nose was small and sharp, and her mouth was full, with the lower lip slightly prominent in a pout. She smelled like the forest—cool, exotic and foreign.

"You're very good," he said, and gave himself a moment to enjoy the way her body held firm and unyielding under his.

"Thanks." She bit the word off, but she didn't struggle. She knew when to fight and when to plot. He outweighed her and he had outfought her, but she wasn't ready to discuss terms of surrender. "I'd appreciate it if you got the hell off me."

"In a minute. Is it your custom to greet people by tossing them on the floor?"

She arched one pale brow. "Is it yours to break into people's homes and poke around in their bedrooms?"

"The door was unlocked," he pointed out. Then he frowned. He was certain he was in the right place, but this was not the woman called Libby. "This is your home?"

"That's right. It's called private property." She struggled not to fidget while he studied her as though she were a particularly interesting specimen in a petri dish. "I've already called the police," she told him, though the closest telephone was ten miles away. "If I were you, I'd make tracks."

"If I wanted to avoid the police, it would be stupid to make tracks." He tilted his head, considering. "And you didn't call them."

"Maybe I did and maybe I didn't." The pout became more pronounced. "What do you want? There's nothing worth stealing in this place."

"I didn't come to steal."

A quick panic, purely feminine, fluttered just below her heart. Fury banked it. "I won't make it easy for you."

"All right." He didn't bother to ask her what she meant. "Who are you?"

"I think I'm entitled to ask you that question," she countered. "And I'm not really interested." Her heart was beginning to thud thickly, and she hoped he couldn't feel it. They were sprawled across the unmade bed, thigh to thigh, as intimately as lovers. His eyes, green and intense, stared into hers until she was breathless all over again.

He saw the panic now, just a flicker of it, and eased his grip on her wrists. Her pulse was beating rapidly there, causing an unexpected reaction to race through him. He could feel it singing through his blood as he shifted his gaze to her mouth.

What would it be like? he wondered. Just a touch, an experiment. A mouth that soft, that full, was designed to tempt a man. Would she fight, or would she yield? Either would prove rewarding. Annoyed by the distraction, he looked into her eyes again. He had a purpose, one he didn't intend to detour from.

"I'm sorry if I startled you, or if I interfered with your privacy. I was looking for someone."

"There's no one here but—" She caught herself and swore under her breath. "Who? Who are you looking for?"

It was best to play it safe, Jacob decided. If he had somehow miscalculated the time, or if Cal's report had been faulty—as they had sometimes been before—it wouldn't be wise to be too specific. "A man. I thought he lived here, but perhaps my information is incorrect."

Sunny blew her bangs out of her eyes. "Who? What's his name?"

"Hornblower," Jacob said, and used his smile for the first time. "His name is Caleb Hornblower." The surprise in Sunny's eyes was all he needed. Instinctively his fingers tightened on her wrists. "You know him?"

Ideas about her sister's somewhat mysterious husband sprang into her mind. He was a spy, a fugitive, an eccentric millionaire on the run. Family loyalty ran deep, and she would rather have had bamboo slivers under her fingernails than betray a loved one.

"Why should I?"

"You know him," Jacob insisted. When her chin came up, he let out a frustrated sigh. "I've come a long way to see him." His lips curved at the understatement. "A very long way. Please, can you tell me where he is?"

When she felt herself softening, she jutted her chin out again. "Obviously he's not here."

"Is he all right?" Jacob released her hands and gripped her shoulders. "Has anything happened to him?"

"No." The very real concern she heard in his voice had her putting a hand over his. "No, of course not. I didn't mean to—" She caught herself again. If this was a trap, she was falling neatly into it. "If you want any information from me, you'll have to tell me who you are and why you want it."

"I'm his brother, Jacob."

Sunny's eyes widened as she let out a long breath.

Cal's brother? It was possible, she supposed. The coloring was similar, and the shape of the face. There was certainly more family resemblance between this man and her brother-in-law than there was between herself and Libby.

"Well," she said after a brief debate with herself, "it really is a small world, isn't it?"

"Smaller than you can imagine. You do know Cal?"

"Yes. Since he married my sister, that makes you and me... I'm not exactly sure what that makes us, but I think we'd be better off discussing it vertically."

He nodded, but he didn't move. "Who are you?"

"Me?" She offered him a big, bright smile. "Oh, I'm Sunbeam." Still smiling, she wrapped her fingers around his thumb. "Now, if you don't want this dislocated, you'll get the hell off my bed."

Chapter 2

They moved apart warily, two boxers retreating to their corners at the sound of the bell. Jacob wasn't entirely sure how to handle her, much less the bombshell she had dropped. His brother was married.

Once they were standing a careful three feet apart, he dipped his hands in the pockets of the comfortable jeans. He noted that, though her stance was easy, she was still braced, ready to counter any move he might attempt. It would have been interesting to make one, just to see what she would do and how she would do it. But he had priorities.

"Where's Cal?"

"Borneo. I think it's Borneo. Might be Bora Bora. Libby's researching a paper." She had time to study him objectively now. Yes, there was a definite resemblance to Cal, in the way he stood, in the rhythm of his speech. But, even though she accepted that, she wasn't ready to trust him. "Cal must have told you she's a cultural anthropologist."

He hesitated, then brought out the smile again. He wasn't nearly as concerned now with what Cal had or had not told him in his report as with what his brother had told this woman named Sunbeam. Sunbeam, he thought distractedly. Was anyone really named Sunbeam?

"Of course." He lied smoothly and without compunction. "He didn't mention he'd be away. How long?"

"A few more weeks." She tugged the red sweater down over her hips. She could already feel bruises forming. It didn't annoy her. She had held her own—well, almost held her own—against him. And she hoped she'd get another shot. "It's funny he never said you were coming."

"He didn't know." Frustrated, he looked out the window at the snow and the trees. He'd come so close, so damn close, only to wait. "I wasn't sure I could make it."

"Yeah." With a lazy shrug, she rocked back on her heels. "Like you couldn't make it to the wedding. We all thought it was odd that none of Cal's family showed up for the big day."

He turned back at that. There was definite censoriousness in her voice. He didn't care for it—he rarely tolerated it—but in this case it was almost amusing. "Believe me, if we could have been here, we would have."

"Hmm. Well, since we've finished wrestling, we might as well go down and have some tea." She started toward the door, flicking a glance over him as she passed. "What degree black belt do you have?"

"Seventh." He cocked an eyebrow. "I didn't want to hurt you."

"Right." More than a little miffed, she started downstairs. "I didn't figure people like you would go in for martial arts."

"People like me?" He spoke absently as he ran his palm over the smooth wood of the railing.

"You're a physicist or something, right?"

"Or something." He spotted a woven throw over the back of a chair in striking colors that challenged rather than blended. Though the look of it tugged at his memory, he resisted the temptation to go over for a closer examination. "And you? What are you?"

"Nothing. I'm working on it."

When Sunny swung into the kitchen, she went directly to the stove. She didn't notice the blank astonishment on Jacob's face.

Like something out of an old video or reference book, he thought as he scanned the room. Only this was much, much better than any reproduction. Delightful, he thought, astonishment turning to pleasure. Absolutely delightful. His hands itched to try out every dial and knob.

"Jacob?"

"What?"

With her brows drawn together, Sunny stared at him. An oddball, she decided. Gorgeous, certainly, but an oddball. And for the time being she was stuck with him. "I said we're big on tea around here. Do you have a preference?"

"No." He couldn't resist. He simply couldn't. As she turned to put the kettle on to boil, he wandered over to the white enameled sink and turned a clunky chrome dial. Water hissed out of the wide-lipped faucet. Holding a finger under the running stream, he discovered it was ice-cold. When he touched the tip of his tongue to his damp finger he detected a faint metallic flavor.

Completely unprocessed water, he decided. Amazing. They drank it exactly as it came out of the ground. Forgetting Sunny, he stuck his finger under again and found that the water had heated enough to make him jolt. Satisfied for the moment, he turned the water off. When he turned back, he saw that Sunny was still standing by the stove. She was staring at him.

There was no use cursing himself, he decided. He

was simply going to have to control his curiosity until he was alone.

"It's very nice," he offered.

"Thanks." Clearing her throat, she kept facing him as she reached behind for the mugs. "We call it a sink. They do have sinks in Philadelphia, don't they?"

"Yes." He took a chance, depending on his research. "I've never used one quite like this."

She relaxed a little. "Well, this place is a throwback."

"I was thinking exactly the same thing."

As the kettle began to sputter, she turned to make the tea. As she worked, she carelessly pushed her sweater up to her elbows. Long, limber arms, he noted. Deceptively fragile in appearance. He rubbed his own forearm. He'd already had a sample of their strength.

"Maybe Cal didn't tell you that my parents built this place in the sixties." She poured steaming water into cups.

"Built it?" he repeated. "Personally?"

"Every stone and log," she told him. "They were hippies. The genuine article."

"The 1960s, yes. I've read about that era. It was a counterculture movement. Youth against the establishment in a political and social revolution that involved a distrust of wealth, government and the military."

"Spoken like a true scientist." A weird one, she added silently as she brought the mugs to the table. "It's funny to hear someone who was born during that time talk about it as if it were as far removed as the Ming dynasty."

Following her lead, he sat down. "Times change."

"Yes." Frowning, she watched as he rubbed a fingertip over the table's surface. "It's called a table," she said helpfully.

He caught himself and picked up the mug. "I was admiring the wood."

"I'm pretty sure it's oak. My father built it, which is why there's a matchbook under one of the legs." At his blank look, she laughed. "He went through a carpentry phase. Almost everything he built in this place wobbles."

He could barely imagine it. Oak split from an actual tree and formed into a piece of furniture. Only those with the highest credit rating could afford the luxury. Even then they were limited by law to a single piece. And here he was, sitting in a house made entirely of wood. He would need samples. It might be difficult with her watching him, distrusting him, but it wasn't impossible.

Thinking it over, he sipped the tea, stopped, then sipped again.

"Herbal Delight."

Sunny lifted her mug in salute. "Right the first time. We could hardly drink anything else without risking a family crisis." With a shake of her head, she studied him over the rim of her mug. "It's my father's company. Didn't Cal tell you that, either?"

"No." Baffled, Jacob stared into the dark, golden tea in his mug. Herbal Delight. Stone. The company, one of the richest and most expansive in the federation, had been established by William Stone. The myths about his beginnings were as romanticized as those about the nineteenth-century president who had been born in a log cabin.

No, not a myth, Jacob thought as the fragrant steam rose from the cup. Reality.

"Just what did Cal tell you?"

Jacob sipped again and struggled for patience. He wanted to record all of this as soon as possible. "Just that he had…flown off course and crashed. Your sister took care of him, and they fell in love." The old resentment welled up in him, and he set down his mug. "And he chose to stay with her, here."

"You have a problem with that?" In a movement that mirrored his, Sunny set down her mug. When they eyed each other now, there was as much dislike as distrust in their looks. "Is that why you didn't bother to show up at the wedding? Because you were annoyed that he decided to get married without clearing it with you?"

His eyes, shades darker as anger grew, snapped to

hers again. "No matter what or how I felt about his decision, I would have been here if it had been possible."

"That's big of you." She shot up to snag a bag of cookies from the pile of groceries. "Let me tell you something, Hornblower. He's lucky to have my sister."

"I wouldn't know."

"I would." Sunny ripped the bag open and dug in. "She's beautiful and brilliant, kind and unselfish." She gestured with half a cookie. "And, if it's any of your business—which it isn't—they're happy together."

"I have no way of knowing that, either."

"Whose fault is that? You've had plenty of time to see them together—if it really mattered to you."

There was fury, rash and dark, in his eyes now. "Time has been the problem." He rose. "All I know is that my brother made a rash decision, a life-altering one. And I intend to make certain it wasn't a mistake."

"You intend?" Sunny choked on a cookie and had to snatch up her mug and drink before she could speak again. "I don't know how things work in your family, pal, but in ours we don't make decisions by committee. We're each considered individuals with the right to choose for ourselves."

He didn't give a damn about her family. He only cared about his own. "My brother's decision affects a great number of people."

"Yeah, I'm sure his marrying Libby is going to

change the course of history." Disgusted, she tossed the bag of cookies back on the counter. "If you're so worried, why the hell has it taken you over a year to put in an appearance?"

"That's my business."

"Oh, I see. That's your business. But my sister's marriage is also your business. You're a real jerk, Hornblower."

"I beg your pardon?"

"I said you're a jerk." She tugged a hand through her hair. "Well, you go right ahead and talk to him when they get back. But there's one thing you haven't put in your calculations. Cal and Libby love each other, which means they belong together. Now, if you'll excuse me, I've got things to do. You can let yourself out."

She stormed off. Moments later, Jacob heard what he imagined was the sound of a primitive wooden door slamming shut.

An exasperating woman, he thought. Interesting, of course, but exasperating. He was going to have to find a way to deal with her, since it was obvious he'd have to extend his stay until Cal's return.

As a scientist, he considered it a tremendous opportunity. To study a primitive culture firsthand, to talk face-to-face with an ancestor—of sorts. He glanced up at the ceiling. He doubted the volatile Sunbeam would appreciate being considered an ancestor.

Yes, it was a tremendous opportunity—scientifically. Personally, he already considered his association with the primitive woman a trial. She was rude, argumentative and aggressive. Perhaps he had the same traits, but he was, after all, superior, being older by several centuries.

The first thing he was going to do when he returned to the ship was open the computer banks and look up what the word *jerk* meant when applied to a man in the twentieth century.

Sunny would have been delighted to give him a concise definition. In fact, as she paced her room she thought of half a dozen more colorful descriptions of his character.

The nerve of the man. To waltz in here more than a year after his brother and her sister married. Not to congratulate them, she thought furiously. Not for a nice family reunion. But to offer his half-baked opinions as to whether Libby was worthy of his brother.

Creep. Jackass. Imbecile.

As she swung past the window, she spotted him down below. Her hand was already on the window sash, prepared to lift the glass so that she could shout the epithets at him. Her anger snapped off as quickly as it had ignited.

Why in the world was he walking into the forest?

Without a coat? Narrowing her eyes, she watched him trudge through the snow toward the sheltering trees. Where the hell was he going? There was nothing in that direction but more trees.

A question sprang into her mind that she'd been too occupied to consider before. How had he gotten here? The cabin was miles from town, and a good two hours' drive from the nearest airport. How the devil had he managed to pop up in her bedroom, coatless, hatless, gloveless, in the middle of winter?

There was no car, no truck, not even a snowmobile, outside the cabin. The idea of him hitchhiking from the highway was ludicrous. A man didn't simply walk into the mountains in January. At least not if he was sane.

With a shudder, she stepped back from the window. Maybe that was the answer. Jacob Hornblower wasn't just a jerk. He was a deranged jerk.

That was an awfully big leap, she told herself. Just because she didn't like him wasn't a good enough reason to assume he was crazy. After all, he was Cal's brother, and over the past year Sunny had become very fond of Cal. Brother Jacob might be an annoying, interfering pain in the neck but that didn't mean he had loose screws.

And yet...

Hadn't she thought he was weird? Hadn't he acted

weird? She looked out the window again, but the only sign of him was the fresh tracks in the snow.

Cal seemed normal enough, she mused, but what did any of them know about his family or his background? Next to nothing. It had always seemed to Sunny that her brother-in-law was strangely closemouthed when it came to his family. She glanced back toward the window again. Maybe he had his reasons.

The man had acted odd right from the start, Sunny decided. The way he'd come into the house unannounced to stand in her bedroom and pore over a copy of *Vogue* as if it were the Dead Sea Scrolls.

Then there was his behavior in the kitchen. Playing with the faucet. And staring. It was as though he'd never seen a stove or refrigerator before. Or hadn't seen one in a very long time. Her mind was jumping like a rabbit. Because he'd been locked up, she thought. Put away where he wasn't a danger to society.

Catching her lip between her teeth, she began to pace again. Her foot connected with his flight bag. Jolting backward, Sunny stared at it. He'd forgotten it. That meant he would be coming back.

Well, she could handle it. She could take care of herself. Rubbing her palms against her thighs, she stared down at the bag. But it wouldn't do any harm to take a few precautions.

Going on impulse, she knelt down. Invasion of privacy or not, she was going to look through the bag. It was odd itself. No zipper or straps. The Velcro peeled apart almost soundlessly. Casting one guilty look over her shoulder, she began to dig.

A change of clothes. Another sweater, black this time. No label. The jeans were soft and obviously expensive, though there was no designer name on the back pocket. No label anywhere. And they were new. She would have sworn they had never been worn. Setting them aside, she pushed deeper. She found a vial marked fluoratyne that contained a clear liquid, and a pair of high-top sneakers in supple leather. No shaving gear, she mused, no mirror. Not even a toothbrush. Just a set of obviously new clothes and a vial that might very well contain some kind of drug.

Her last discovery was the most puzzling of all. An electronic device, no bigger than the palm of her hand, was tucked in the corner of the bag. Circular in shape, it was hinged back. When she opened it she saw a series of tiny buttons. After touching the first, she jumped back at the sound of Jacob's voice.

As clear as a bell, it came from the circle of metal in her hand. He was reciting equations, as far as she could tell. Neither the numbers nor the terms meant anything to her. But the fact that they were emitted by the little disk opened up new realms of possibility.

He was a spy. Probably for the other side. Whatever

the other side was. And from his behavior it was natural to assume that he was an unbalanced spy. Imagination had never been Sunny's weak point. She could see it all perfectly.

He had been captured. Whatever techniques had been used to pull information from him had unhinged his mind. Cal had covered for him, making up a story about his brother being an astrophysicist, too deep in research to travel to the West Coast, when in reality he had been in some sort of federal institution. And now he'd escaped.

Sunny pushed buttons at random until Jacob's voice clicked off. She would have to treat him carefully. Whatever her personal feelings, he was family. She'd have to make absolutely certain he was a dangerous lunatic before she did anything about it.

A stupid, often annoying person. Jacob scowled at the puff of smoke he saw through the last line of trees. He didn't care for the definition of *jerk*. Being called annoying didn't bother him in the least. But stupid did. He would not tolerate some skinny woman who considered the combustion engine the height of technology calling him stupid.

He'd gotten quite a bit done overnight. His ship was well camouflaged, and his records had been brought up to date. Including his infuriating encounter with

Sunbeam Stone. It hadn't been until sunrise that he'd remembered his flight bag.

If she hadn't made him lose his temper, he would never have left it behind. Not that it contained anything valuable. It was the principle of the thing. He was not absentminded by nature, and he only forgot minor details when his mind was absorbed with larger ones.

And he resented thinking of her. She had popped into his mind on and off as he'd worked through the night. A constant annoyance—like an itch on the shoulder blade that was just out of reach. How she'd crouched, ready to fight, chin up, body braced. How that body had felt under his, tensed, challenging. How her hair glowed, like her name.

Furious, he shook his head, as if to dislodge her from his thoughts. He didn't have time for women. It wasn't that he didn't appreciate them, but there was a time for pleasure. This wasn't it. And if it was pleasure he wanted, Sunbeam Stone was not where he should look for it.

The more he thought about where he was, when he was, the more he was certain that Cal needed to be brought to his senses and taken home.

Some sort of space fever, Jacob decided. His brother had suffered a shock, and the woman—as some women had throughout time—had taken advantage of him.

When he approached Cal logically, they would get into the ship and go home.

In the meantime, he would take the opportunity to study and record at least this small section of the world.

At the edge of the forest, he paused. It was colder today, and he sincerely regretted the lack of warmer clothing. Gray clouds, plump with snow, had drifted in to cover the sun. In the gloomy light he watched Sunny lifting logs from the woodpile at the rear of the cabin. She was singing in a powerfully erotic voice about a man who had gotten away. She didn't hear his approach, and she continued to sing and stack wood in her arms.

"Excuse me."

With a yelp, she jumped back, sending the split logs flying. One landed hard on her booted foot, and she swore roundly and hopped up and down. "Damn it! Damn, damn, damn! What's wrong with you?" Clasping her wounded foot with one hand, she braced the other on the cabin wall.

"Nothing." He couldn't help the grin. "I think there's something wrong with you. Does it hurt?"

"No, it feels great. I live for pain." She gritted her teeth as she set her foot gingerly back on the ground. "Where did you come from?"

"Philadelphia." She narrowed her eyes. "Oh, you mean now?" With a jerk of his thumb, he said, "That way." He paused to glance at the logs scattered in the snow. "Want some help?"

"No." Favoring her foot, she crouched down to retrieve the logs. All the while, she watched him carefully, braced for any move he might make. "Do you know why I'm here, Hornblower? For peace and solitude." She blew the hair out of her eyes as she looked up at him. "Do you understand the concepts?"

"Yes."

"Good." Turning, she limped back into the cabin, letting the door slam shut behind her. After dumping the logs in the woodbox, she came back to the kitchen. And swore. "What now?"

"I left my bag." He sniffed the air. "Is something burning?"

With a sound of disgust, she darted to the toaster, banging on it until the smoking, blackened bread popped up. "This stupid thing sticks."

To get a better look at the fascinating little device, he leaned over her shoulder. "Doesn't look appetizing."

"It's fine." To prove it, she bit into the toast.

Her scent drifted to him over the smoke. His instant reaction annoyed him, but pride had him resisting the instinctive move away. "Are you always so stubborn?"

"Yes."

"And so unfriendly?"

"No."

She turned and was immediately made aware of the miscalculation. He didn't move aside, as she had expected. Instead, he leaned forward, resting his palms against the counter and casually caging her between his arms. There was nothing she detested more than being outmaneuvered.

"Back off, Hornblower."

"No." He did shift, but closer. As on their first meeting, their thighs rubbed, but there was nothing lover-like in the connection. "You interest me, Sunbeam."

"Sunny," she said automatically. "Don't call me Sunbeam."

"You interest me," he repeated. "Do you consider yourself an average woman of your time?"

Baffled, she shook her head. "What kind of a question is that?"

She had dozens of shades in her hair, from pale white to dark honey. He was sorry he had noticed. "One that requires a simple answer. Do you?"

"No. No one likes to be considered average. Now would you—"

"You're beautiful." His gaze skimmed over her face, deliberately, a test of himself and his endurance. "But that's merely physical. What do you think separates you from the average?"

"What are you doing, a thesis?" She lifted a hand to

shove him away and met the solid wall of his chest. She could feel his heartbeat there, slow and steady.

"More or less." He smiled. He was disturbing her at a very basic level, and he found it intensely satisfying.

It was his eyes, Sunny thought. Even if the man was unhinged, he had the most incredibly hypnotic eyes. "I thought you dealt with planets and stars, not with people."

"People live on planets."

"At least this one."

He smiled again. "At least. You could consider this a personal interest."

She wanted to shift but realized that would only make the contact more intimate. Cursing him, she kept her voice and her gaze level. "I don't want your personal interest, Jacob."

"J.T." He felt the quick tremor from her body into his. "The family usually calls me J.T."

"All right." She spoke slowly, all too aware that her brain had turned to mush. What she needed was some distance. "How about you get out of my way, J.T., and I put together some breakfast?"

If she didn't stop nibbling on her lip, he was going to have to stop her in the most effective way he knew. He hadn't realized that such a small, nervous habit could be seductive. "Is that an invitation?"

Her tongue slipped out to nurse her lip. "Sure."

He leaned closer, enjoying the way her eyes widened, darkened, steadied. It wasn't easy to resist. He was known for his brilliance, his tenacity, his temper. But not for his control. And he wanted to kiss her, not scientifically, not experimentally. Ruthlessly.

"Toast!" he murmured.

She let out a quick puff of air. "Froot Loops. They're great. My favorite."

He eased back, much more for his sake than for hers. If he was going to spend the next few weeks around her, he was going to have to work on that control. Because he had a plan.

"I could use some breakfast."

"Fine." Telling herself it was a change of strategy, not a retreat, she darted across the kitchen to pluck two bowls from the cupboard. With those and a colorful box in hand, she walked to the table. "We could never have these as kids. My mother was—is—a health fiend. Her idea of cold cereal is hunks of roots and tree bark."

"Why would she choose to eat tree bark?"

"Don't ask me." Sunny grabbed the milk from the fridge, then dumped it over the piles of colorful circles. "Anyway, ever since I moved out I've been on a binge of junk food. I figure since I ate healthy for the first twenty years I can poison myself for the next twenty."

"Poison," he repeated, giving the cereal a dubious look.

"To the health fiend, sugar's poison. Dig in," she added, offering him a spoon. "Burnt toast and cold cereal are my specialties." She smiled, charmingly. She, too, had a plan.

Because he wouldn't have put it past her to poison him, he waited until she had begun to eat before he sampled the cereal. Soggy candy, he decided. And fairly appealing. He considered the informal meal a good start if he wanted to ingratiate himself with her enough to pump her for information.

It was obvious that Cal had told no one except Libby about where—and when—he had come from. Jacob gave him full marks for that. It was better all around if the matter was kept quiet. The repercussions would be...well, he had yet to calculate them. But Sunny might not have been far off when she had said that Cal's marrying her sister could change the course of history.

So he would play the game close, and cautious, and use the situation to his advantage. Use her to his advantage, he thought with only a twinge of guilt.

He intended to pick her brain, about her family, her sister in particular, her impressions of Cal. And he wanted her firsthand account of life in the twentieth century. With a little luck, he might be able to convince her to guide him into the nearest city, where he could add to his data.

It wouldn't do to lose her temper with him, Sunny thought. If she wanted to find out exactly who and what he was, she would have to employ more tact. It wasn't her strong point, but she could learn. She was as completely alone with him as it was possible to be. And, since she had no intention of packing up and leaving, she would just have to exercise some caution and some diplomacy. Particularly if he was as loony as she believed.

It was too bad that he was crazy, she thought, smiling at him. Anyone that attractive, that blatantly sexy, deserved a solid, working brain. Maybe it was only a temporary mental breakdown.

"So." She tapped her spoon against the side of her bowl. "What do you think of Oregon so far?"

"It's very big—and underpopulated."

"That's how we like it." She let the lull drag out. "Did you fly into Portland?"

He wavered between a lie and the truth. "No, my transportation brought me a bit closer. Do you live here with Cal and your sister?"

"No. I have a place in Portland, but I'm thinking of giving it up."

"To what?"

"Just giving it up." She shot him a puzzled look, then shrugged. "Actually, I'm toying with the idea of going east for a while. New York."

"To do what?"

"I haven't decided."

He set his spoon aside. "You have no work?"

Automatically her shoulders squared. "I'm in between jobs. I recently resigned from a managerial position in retail." She'd been fired from her job as assistant manager of the lingerie department of a midlevel department store. "I'm considering going back to school for a law degree."

"Law?" His eyes softened. There was something so appealing about the look that she nearly smiled at him and meant it. "My mother is in law."

"Really? I don't think Cal mentioned it. What kind of law does she practice?"

Because he thought it would be a bit difficult to explain his mother's position, he asked, "What kind did you have in mind?"

"I'm leaning toward criminal law." She started to elaborate, then stopped herself. She didn't want to talk about herself but about him. "It's funny, isn't it, that my sister should be a scientist and Cal's brother should be one? Just what does an astrophysicist do?"

"Theorizes. Experiments."

"About stuff like interplanetary travel?" She tried not to smirk but didn't quite succeed. "You don't really believe all that stuff—like people flying off to Venus the way they fly to Cleveland?"

It was fortunate he was a cool hand at poker. His face remained bland as he continued to eat. "Yes."

She laughed indulgently. "I guess you have to, but

isn't it frustrating to go into all that knowing that even if it becomes possible it won't happen in your lifetime?"

"Time's relative. In the early part of this century a flight to the moon was considered implausible. But it has been done." Clumsily, he thought, but it had been done. "In the next century man goes to Mars and beyond."

"Maybe." She got up to take two bottles of soda from the refrigerator. "But it would be hard for me to devote my life to something I'd never see happen." As Jacob watched in fascination, she took a small metal object out of a drawer, applied it like a lever to the top of each bottle and dislodged the caps. "I guess I like to see results, and see them now," she admitted as she set the first bottle in front of him. "Instant gratification. Which is why I'm twenty-three and between jobs."

The bottle was glass, Jacob mused. The same kind she had tried to strike him with the afternoon before. Lifting it, he sipped. He was pleasantly surprised by the familiar taste. He enjoyed the same soft drink at home, though it wasn't his habit to drink it for breakfast.

"Why did you decide to study space?"

He glanced back at her. He recognized a grilling when he heard one, and he thought it would be entertaining to both humor and annoy her. "I like possibilities."

"You must have studied a long time."

"Long enough." He sipped again.

"Where?"

"Where what?"

She managed to keep the pleasant smile intact. "Where did you study?"

He thought of the Kroliac Institute on Mars, the Birmington University in Houston and his brief and intense year in the L'Espace Space Laboratory in the Fordon Quadrant. "Here and there. At the moment I'm attached to a small private facility outside of Philadelphia."

She wondered if the staff of that private facility wore white coats. "I guess you find it fascinating."

"Only more so recently. Are you nervous?"

"Why?"

"You keep tapping your foot."

She placed a hand on her knee to stop the movement. "Restless. I get restless if I stay in one place too long." It was obvious, painfully so, that she wasn't going to get anywhere with him this way. "Listen, I really do have some things to…" Her words trailed off as she glanced out the window. She didn't know when the snow had begun, but it was coming down in sheets. "Terrific."

Following her gaze, Jacob studied the thick white flakes. "Looks like it means business."

"Yeah." She let out her breath in a sigh. Maybe he did make her nervous, but she wasn't a monster. "And it's not the kind of weather suitable for camping in the woods." Fighting with her conscience, she walked to the door, back to the table, then to the window. "Look, I know you don't have a place to stay. I saw you walk into the forest yesterday."

"I have…all I need."

"Sure, but I can't have you go trudging into the hills in a blizzard to sleep in a tent or something. Libby would never forgive me if you died of exposure." Thrusting her hands in her pockets, she scowled at him. "You can stay here."

He considered the possibilities and smiled. "I'd love to."

Chapter 3

He stayed out of her way. It seemed the best method of handling the situation for the moment. She'd stationed herself on the sofa by the fire, books heaped beside her, and was busily taking notes. A portable radio sat on the table, crackling with static and music and the occasional weather report. Absorbed in her research, Sunny ignored him.

Taking advantage of the opportunity, Jacob explored his new quarters. She'd given him the room next to hers—larger by a couple of meters, with a pair of paned windows facing southeast. The bed was a big, boxy affair framed in wood, with a spring-type mattress that creaked when he sat on the edge.

There was a shelf crowded with books, novels and poetry of the nineteenth and twentieth centuries. They were paperbacks, for the most part, with bright, eye-catching covers. He recognized one or two of the names. He flipped through them with an interest that was more scientific than literary. It was Cal, he thought, who read for pleasure, who had a talent for retaining little bits of prose and poetry. It was rare for Jacob to while away an hour of his time with fiction.

They were still using trees to make the pages of books, he remembered with a kind of dazed fascination. One side had cut them down to make room for housing and to make furniture and paper and fuel, while the other side had scurried to replant them. Never quite catching up.

It had been an odd sort of game, one of many that had led to incredible and complicated environmental problems.

Then, of course, they'd saturated the air with carbon dioxide, gleefully punching holes in the ozone, then fluttering their hands when faced with the consequences. He wondered what kind of people poisoned their own air. And water, he recalled with a shake of his head. Another game had been to throw whatever was no longer useful into the ocean, as if the seas were a bottomless dumping ground. It was fortunate that they had begun to get the picture before the damage had become irreparable.

Turning from the window, he wandered the room,

running a fingertip along the walls, over the bedspread, the bedposts. Certainly the textures were interesting, and yet…

He paused when he spotted a picture framed in what appeared to be silver. The frame itself would have caught his attention, but it was the picture that drew him. His brother, smiling. He was wearing a tuxedo and looking very pleased with himself. His arm was around the woman called Libby. She had flowers in her hair and wore a white full-sleeved dress that laced to the throat.

A wedding dress, Jacob mused. In his own time the ceremony was coming back into style after having fallen into disfavor in the latter part of the previous century. Couples were finding a new pleasure in the old traditions. It had no basis in logic, of course. There was a contract to seal a marriage, and a contract to end one. Each was as easily forged as the other. But elaborate weddings were in fashion once more.

Churches were once again the favored atmosphere for the exchange of rings and vows. Designers were frantically copying gowns from museums and old videos. The gown Libby wore would have drawn moans of envy from those who admired the fuss and bother of marriage rites.

He couldn't imagine it. The entire business puzzled him, and it would have amused him if not for the fact that it involved his brother. Not Cal, who had always been enamored of women in general but never of one in particular. The idea of Cal being matched was illogical. And yet he was holding the proof in his hand.

It infuriated him.

To have left his family, his home, his world. And for a woman. Jacob slammed the picture down on the dresser and turned away. It had been madness. There was no other explanation. One woman couldn't change a life so drastically. And what else was there here to tempt a man? Oh, it was an interesting place, certainly. Fascinating enough to warrant a few weeks of study and research. He would undoubtedly write a series of papers on the experience when he returned to his own time. But…what was the ancient saying? A nice place to visit, but I wouldn't want to live there.

He would put Caleb in his right mind again. Whatever the woman had done to him he would undo. No one knew Caleb Hornblower better than his own brother.

They had been together not so long ago. Time was relative, he thought again, but without humor. The last evening they had spent together had been in Jacob's quarters at the university. They'd played poker and drank Venusian rum—a particularly potent liquor manufactured on the neighboring planet. Cal had commandeered an entire case from his last run.

As Jacob remembered, Cal had lost at cards, cheerfully and elaborately, as was his habit.

They had both gotten sloppy drunk.

"When I get back from this run," Cal had said, tipping back in his chair and yawning hugely, "I'm going to spend three weeks on the beach—south of France, I think—watching women and staying drunk."

"Three days," Jacob had told him. He'd swirled the coal-black liquor in his glass. "Then you'd go up again. In the last ten years you've been in the air more than on the ground."

"You don't fly enough." With a grin, Cal had taken Jacob's glass and downed the contents. "Stuck in your lab, little brother. I tell you it's a lot more fun to bounce around the planets than to study them."

"Point of view. If I didn't study them, you couldn't bounce around them." He had slid down in his chair, too lazy to pour himself more rum. "Besides, you're a better pilot than I am. It's the only thing you do better than I do."

Cal had grinned again. "Point of view," he had tossed back. "Ask Linsy McCellan."

Jacob had stirred himself enough to raise a brow. That particular woman, a dancer, had generously shared her attributes with both men—on separate occasions. "She's too easily entertained." His smile had turned wicked. "In any case, I'm here, on the ground, with her, a great deal more than you are."

"Even Linsy—" he lifted his glass "—bless her, can't compete with flying."

"With running cargo, Cal? If you'd stayed with the ISF you'd be a major by now."

Cal had only shrugged. "I'll leave the regimentation for you, Dr. Hornblower." Then he had sat up, sluggish from drink but still eager. "J.T., why don't you give this place the shake for a few weeks and come with me? There's this club in the Brigston Colony on Mars that needs to be seen to be believed. There's this mutant sax player— Anyhow, you've got to be there."

"I've got work."

"You've always got work," Cal had pointed out. "A couple of weeks, J.T. Fly up with me. I can make the transport, show you a few of the seedier parts of the colony, then I can call in to base before we watch those women on the beach. You just have to name the beach."

It had been tempting, so tempting that Jacob had nearly agreed. The impulse had been there, as always. But so had the responsibilities. "Can't." Heaving a sigh, he'd lunged for the bottle again. "I have to finish these equations before the first of the month."

He should have gone, Jacob thought now. He should have said the hell with the equations, with the responsibilities, and jumped ship with Cal. Maybe it wouldn't have happened if he'd been along. Or, if it had, at least he would have been there, with his brother.

The video report on Cal's wounded ship had shown exactly what Cal had been through. The black hole, the panic, the helplessness as he'd been sucked toward the void and battered by its gravitational field. That he had survived at all was a miracle, and a tribute to his skill as a pilot. But if he'd had a scientist on board he might have avoided the rest. And he would be home now. They would both be home. Where they belonged.

Calming himself, he turned from the window. In a few weeks, they would be. All he had to do was wait.

To pass the time, he began to toy with the clunky computer sitting on the desk in the corner. For an hour he amused himself with it, dismantling the keyboard and putting it together again, examining switches and circuits and chips. For his own entertainment he slipped one of Libby's disks into the drive.

It was a long, involved report on some remote tribe in the South Pacific. Despite himself, Jacob found himself caught up in the descriptions and theories. She had a way of turning dry facts about a culture into a testament to the people who made it. It was ironic that she had focused on the effects of modern tools and technology on what was to her a primitive society. He had spent a great deal of time over the last year wondering what effect the technology he had at his fingertips would have on her time and place.

She was intelligent, he admitted grudgingly. She was obviously thorough and precise when it came to her work. Those were qualities he could admire. But that didn't mean she could keep his brother.

Shutting the machine down, he went back downstairs.

Sunny didn't bother to look up when she heard him come down the stairs. She wanted to think she'd forgotten he was there at all as she'd pored over her law books. But she hadn't. She couldn't complain that he was noisy or made a nuisance of himself. Except that he did make a nuisance of himself just by being there.

Because she wanted to be alone, she told herself as she glanced up and watched him stroll into the kitchen. That wasn't true. She hated to be alone for long periods of time. She liked people and conversation, arguments and parties. But he bothered her. Tapping her pen against her pad, she studied the fire. Why? That was the big question.

Possibly loony, she wrote on her pad. Then she grinned to herself. Actually, it was more than possible that he'd had a clearance sale on the top floor. Popping out of nowhere, living in the forest, playing with faucets.

Possibly dangerous. That turned her grin into a

scowl. There weren't many men who could get past her guard the way he had. But he hadn't hurt her, and she had to admit he'd had the opportunity. Still, there was a difference between dangerous and violent.

Forceful personality. There was an intensity about him that couldn't be ignored. Even when he was quiet, watchful in that strange way of his, he seemed to be charged. A live wire ready to shock. Then he would smile, unexpectedly, disarmingly, and you were willing to risk the jolt.

Wildly attractive. Sunny didn't like the phrase, but it suited him too well for her not to use it. There was something ruthless and untamed in his looks—the lean, almost predatory face and the mane of dark hair. And his eyes, that deep, dark green that seemed to look straight into you. The heavy lids didn't give them a sleepy look, but a brooding one.

Heathcliff, she thought, and laughed at herself. It was Libby who was the romantic one. Libby would always look into a person's heart. Sunny would always be compelled to dissect the brain.

Absently she sketched his face on a corner of the paper. There was something different about him, she mused as she penciled in the dark brows and the heavy lashes. It bothered her that she couldn't put her finger on it. He was evasive, secretive, eccentric. She could accept all that—once she discovered what he was evading. Was he in trouble? Had he done something that re-quired him to pack up quickly and find a place, a quiet, remote place, to hide?

Or was it really as simple as he said? He had come to see his brother and to get a firsthand look at his brother's wife.

No. Scowling down at the impromptu portrait, Sunny shook her head. That might be the truth, but it was no more than half of it. J.T. Hornblower was up to some-thing. And, sooner or later, she was going to find out what it was.

With a shrug, she set her pad aside. That was reason enough for her interest in Jacob Hornblower. She only wanted to know what made the man tick. With that in mind, she rose and went into the kitchen.

"What in the hell are you doing?"

Jacob glanced up. Spread all over the table in front of him were the various parts of the toaster and a car-pet of crumbs. He'd found a screwdriver in a drawer and was having the time of his life.

"It needs to be fixed."

"Yes, but—"

"Do you like your bread burned?"

She narrowed her eyes. His fingers, long, lean and clever, skimmed over screws. "Do you know what you're doing?"

"Maybe." He smiled, wondering what she would say

if he told her he could dismantle an X-25 primary unit in under an hour. "Don't you trust me?"

"No." She turned to put on the kettle. "But I don't suppose you can make it any worse than it already is." Friendly, she reminded herself. She would be friendly and casual, then move in for the kill. "Want some tea?"

"Sure." With the screwdriver in his hand, he watched her walk from stove to cupboard and back to stove. Grace, he thought, when combined with strength, was an appealing combination. She had a way of shifting her weight so that her whole body flowed into the movement. Yet there was a control about her, the kind of discipline seen in athletes and dancers. And it wasn't genderless, but innately and completely female.

When the nerves at the back of her neck began to prickle, she glanced over her shoulder. "Problem?"

"No. I like to watch you."

Because she didn't have a ready response for that, she poured the tea. "Want a cupcake?"

"Okay."

She tossed him a little chocolate cake wrapped in clear paper. "If you want something more elaborate for lunch, you're on your own." She brought the cups to the table, then sat across from him. "How are you with plumbing?"

"Excuse me?"

"The faucet in the tub leaks." Sunny tore the paper

from her cupcake. "My solution's been to put a wash-rag on the drain to muffle the noise at night, but if you're handy there's probably a wrench around some-where." She took the first bite, closing her eyes to bet-ter enjoy the taste. "We could consider it a trade-off for your meals."

"I can take a look." He was still holding the screw-driver, but he was more interested in the way she gently licked icing from the cake. It had never occurred to him that eating could be quite so sexy. "Do you live alone?"

She lifted a brow, then nipped at the cake again. "Obviously."

"When you're not here."

"Most of the time." She sucked chocolate from her finger and had his stomach clenching. "I like living alone, not having to check with anyone if I want to eat at ten or go dancing at midnight. Do you?"

"What?"

"Live alone?"

"Yes. My work takes up most of my time."

"Physics, right? Too bad." She settled back with her tea. The idea of him being a spy was beginning to sound absurd. And, to give him his due, she decided, he wasn't as crazy as she'd initially believed. Eccen-tric, she thought. If there was one thing Sunny under-stood, it was eccentricity. She'd lived with it all of her life. "So you really like splitting atoms, or whatever it is you guys do?"

"Something like that."

"What's your stand on nuclear reactors?"

He nearly laughed, but then he remembered where he was. "Nuclear fission is like trying to dispose of a mouse with a rocket launcher. Dangerous and unnecessary."

"My mother would love you, but that doesn't sound very physicist-like."

"Not all scientists agree." Knowing he was on unsteady ground, he went back to the toaster. "Tell me about your sister."

"Libby? Why?"

"I have an interest in her, since she has my brother."

"She isn't exactly holding him for ransom," Sunny said dryly. "In fact, he rushed her down the aisle so fast, she barely had time to say 'I do.'"

"What aisle?"

"It's a figure of speech, J.T." She spoke slowly now, and with a sigh. "When people get married, they, you know, go down the aisle."

"Oh, right." He thought that over as he fiddled with the toaster. "You're saying that the marriage was Cal's idea."

"I don't know whose idea it was, if that matters, but he was certainly enthusiastic." Her fingers began to drum as her annoyance grew. "I get the impression you think Libby pushed Cal into something here, or that she, I don't know, used feminine wiles to trap him."

"Does she have them?"

After she finished choking on her tea, Sunny took a long breath. "This may be tough for you to understand, Hornblower, but Cal and Libby love each other. You've heard of love, haven't you? Or doesn't it compute?"

"I've heard of the concept," he said, mildly enough. It was intriguing to watch her temper rise—as it did with very little provocation. Her eyes darkened, her skin flushed, her chin lifted. Attractive when composed, she was simply devastating when aroused. He wouldn't have been human if he hadn't considered how interesting it would be to arouse her in other, more rewarding ways. "I haven't experienced it myself, but I have an open mind."

"That's big of you," she muttered. Rising, she stuffed her hands in the back pockets of her jeans and stalked to the window. Lord, he was a prize. If she managed to keep from murdering him before Cal and Libby got back, it would be a miracle.

"Have you?"

"Have I what?"

"Been in love," he said, running the staff of the screwdriver through his fingers.

She sent him a particularly vicious look. "Keep out of my personal life."

"I'm sorry." He wasn't, not a bit. He was as determined to make her look like a fool as she was to make him sound like one. "It's just that you sounded so knowledgeable on the subject I assumed you'd had quite a bit of experience. Yet you're not matched—married—are you?"

Whether he'd aimed or just shot from the hip, he'd hit the target dead-on. She hadn't been in love, though she'd tried to be several times. Self-doubt only fanned the flames of anger.

"Just because a person hasn't been in love doesn't mean he or she can't appreciate its value." She whirled back, hating the fact that she'd been put on the defensive and determined to turn the conversation around. "The fact that I'm not married is purely a personal choice."

"I see."

The way he said it had her teeth snapping together. "And this has nothing to do with me. We're talking about Libby and Cal."

"I thought we were talking about love as a concept."

"Talking about love with a heartless clod is a waste of time, and I never waste mine." She balled a hand on her hip. "But we both have an interest in Libby and Cal, so we'll clear it up."

"All right." He tapped the screwdriver on the edge of

the table. He didn't need a computer to tell him what a clod was. It was just one more thing she would have to pay for before this was over. "Clear it up."

"You automatically assume that my sister, being a woman, lured your brother, being only a man, into marriage. What an incredibly outdated theory."

His fingers paused in the act of reattaching the toaster's coil. "Is it?"

"Incredibly outdated, chauvinistic and stupid. The idea that all women want is marriage and a house with a picket fence went out with the poodle skirt."

Though he wondered who in his right mind would put skirts on poodles, there was something more important to touch on. "Stupid?" he repeated.

"Idiotic." Legs spread, jaw firm, she baited him. "Only a true idiot would be alive today with that kind of Neanderthal attitude. Maybe the last few decades have passed you by, pal, but things have changed." She was on a roll now, a slender steamroller with right on her side. "Women have choices today, options, alternatives. An enlightened few even figure that, because they do, men benefit from the same expanding horizons. Except, of course, men like you, who are mired in their own self-importance."

He stood at that, in a slow, deliberate manner that would have tipped her off if she hadn't been so angry. "I'm not mired in anything."

"You're up to your neck in it, Hornblower. From the minute you got here you've been trying to find some way to turn your brother's marriage into a set-up created by my sister." She took one long-legged stride toward him. "I've got a flash for you. Only a fool gets tricked into marriage, and Cal doesn't strike me as a fool. That's where the family resemblance fades."

A jerk, a clod, an idiot and now a fool. Yes, he thought, she was going to pay. "Then why did he marry so quickly, without even attempting to come home and see his family first?"

"You'll just have to ask him," she shot back. "It could be because he didn't want to be questioned or hounded or interrogated. In my family we don't pressure the people we love. And in the real world women get along just fine without setting snares for unwary men. The fact is, Hornblower, we don't need you."

This time it was he who took the step. "You don't?"

"No. Not for winning the bread or chopping the wood, running the country or taking out the garbage. Or—or fixing toasters," she added, with a wild gesture toward the mess on the table. "We can do everything we need to do just dandy on our own."

"You left out something."

Her chin lifted a fraction higher. "What?"

His hand clamped quickly around the back of her neck. Sunny had time for a hiss of surprise before his mouth closed over hers. When a woman was expecting a left to the jaw, she had little defense against a heated embrace.

She murmured something. He felt her lips move beneath his. His name, he thought, as the whisper of sound and movement shuddered into him. He was angry—more than angry—but his hair-trigger temper had never taken him so deep into trouble before.

And she was trouble. He'd known it from the first glimpse.

Recklessly he ignored logic and consequences and dragged her closer. Her hands had shot out of her pockets, and now they were clenched taut as wire on his shoulders, neither resisting nor surrendering. He wanted, craved, one or the other. With an oath he nipped at her full, seductive lower lip until her gasp of pleasure shocked the air.

She'd been right about the high-powered voltage that ran through him. Her system was jolted again and again as he held her closer, tighter, harder. She didn't struggle. For, while her body was charged with the current that raced from him into her, her mind emptied, thoughts streaming away like colored chalk in the rain.

She felt his muscles tense under her fingers, heard his sharp intake of breath as she pressed herself more fully against him. She could taste the passion, riper, darker, than any she had ever known, but she couldn't be sure if it was his or her own.

It was as if she had come alive in his arms. He felt her go from rigid shock to molten aggression in the space of a heartbeat. Of all the women he had pleasured, or been pleasured by, he had never known one who matched him so perfectly. Passion to passion, demand to demand.

He ran his hands through her short cap of hair. Warm silk. Down the slender curve of her throat. Hot satin. With his tongue he sampled the potent flavors of her mouth, and then he groaned as she drew him deeper into her.

Never had need spun so quickly out of control, risen so high above the tolerable.

He hurt. And he had never hurt before, not from wanting. He reeled, the way a man might stagger from lack of food or sleep. And he knew fear—a sharp and sudden terror that his own destiny had been removed neatly from his hands.

It was that which had him yanking her away, his fingers biting into her arms as he held her back. His breath came fast and shallow, as if he had raced to the top of a cliff. Indeed, staring at her, he thought he could see the drop, spread below him like a vision of jagged rocks and boiling seas.

She said nothing, just stared with eyes that were huge

and dark. In the milky winter light her skin was pale and clear. Like a statue, she stood utterly still, utterly silent. Then she began to tremble.

Jacob snatched his hands away as if he'd been burned.

"I suppose…" Because her voice was weak, Sunny took a long, cleansing breath. "I suppose that was your way of proving a point."

He pushed his hands into his pockets and felt exactly like what she had called him. A fool. "It was a choice between that and a left jab."

Either way, he'd scored a knockout. Steadier now, she nodded. "If you're going to stay here for the time being, we're going to have to establish some rules."

She recovered quickly, he thought, with a bitterness that surprised him. "Yours, I suppose."

"Yes." She wanted to sit down, badly, but forced herself to face him eye-to-eye. "We can argue all you like. In fact, I enjoy a good argument."

"You're seductive when you argue."

She opened her mouth, then closed it again. No one had ever accused her of that. "I guess you'll just have to learn how to control yourself."

"It's not my strong suit."

"Or take a hike in what's already over a foot of snow."

He glanced toward the window. "I'll work on it."

"Fair enough." She took another long breath. "Though

it's obvious we don't like each other very much, we can try to be civil as long as we're stuck with each other."

"Nicely put." He wanted to trace a finger down her cheek but wisely resisted the temptation. "Can I ask you a question?"

"All right."

"Do you usually respond so radically to men you don't like?"

"That's none of your business." Temper brought a flattering tinge of color to her cheeks.

"I thought it was a very civil question." Then he smiled and changed tactics. "But I'll retract it, because if we argue again so soon we'll just end up in bed."

"Of all the—"

"Are you willing to chance it?" he said quietly. He gave a slow, satisfied nod when she subsided. "I thought not. If it makes you feel any better, neither am I." So saying, he sat and picked up the tools again. "Why don't we just cross the whole business off as poor judgment."

"You were the one who—"

"Yes." He looked up, his gaze carefully neutral. "I was."

It was pride that had her stalking toward the table when she would have preferred to slink away and nurse her wounds. "And I suppose it's asking too much to expect an apology."

"I don't need one," he said easily.

She snatched up a toaster part and flung it. "You're the one who did the manhandling, Hornblower."

With difficulty, he checked himself. If he touched her again, now, they would both regret it. "All right. I'm sorry I kissed you, Sunny." There was an edge to his voice as his eyes whipped up to hers. "I can't begin to tell you how sorry."

She spun around and stormed out of the room. The apology hadn't mollified her. In fact, it had only inflated an angry hurt. She picked up the heaviest book she could find and flung it across the room. She kicked the sofa, swore, then streaked up the steps.

It didn't help. None of it helped. The fury was still roiling inside her. And worse, much worse, was the need, the raw-edged need, that tangled with it. He'd done that, she thought, slamming the door. Deliberately, too. She was sure of it.

He'd managed to make her so angry, to push her so close to the edge, that she'd responded irrationally when he'd kissed her.

It wouldn't happen again—that she promised herself. Humiliation was nearly as bad as being outmaneuvered, and he'd managed to do both in a matter of hours. He was going to have to pay for it.

Throwing herself down on the bed, she decided to spend the rest of the afternoon devising ways to make Jacob Hornblower's life a living hell.

Chapter 4

He never should have touched her. Jacob cursed himself. Then he found that it was much more convenient, and much more satisfying, to curse her. She'd started it, after all. He'd known, right from the start, that she would make trouble for him.

There were some people in this world—in any world, he thought bitterly—who were just born to complicate other people's lives. Sunbeam Stone was one of them. In her looks, in her voice, in her gestures, in her personality, she had everything a woman needed to distract a man. To aggravate him to the edge of reason. And beyond.

She challenged him at every meeting. Those cool smiles, that hot temper. It was a combination he couldn't resist. And he was sure she knew it.

When he'd kissed her—and God knew he hadn't meant to—it had been like being shot into hyperspace without a ship. How could he have known that damn sulky mouth of hers would be so potent?

He'd never been attracted to passive women. But what difference did that make? He had no intention of being attracted to Sunny. He couldn't be. He damn well wouldn't be, no matter what tricks she pulled out of her twentieth-century hat.

What had happened was completely her fault, he decided. She'd taunted and tempted him. She'd wanted to confuse him. Gritting his teeth, he admitted that she'd done a brilliant job of it. After she had and he'd reacted as any normal man would, she'd looked at him with those big, gorgeous eyes full of panic and passion. Oh, she was a case, all right. His study of the twentieth century should have warned him that women had been much more bewildering back then. And craftier.

Hands in pockets, he paced to the window to watch the swirling snow. Oh, she was a bright one, he mused. Sharp as Venusian crystal, and twice as deadly. She knew something wasn't quite right about his story, and she was determined to find out just what he was holding back. And he was just as determined to keep her in the dark.

In a battle of wits, he had every confidence his would prevail. How much effort would it take to outwit a twentieth-century woman? After all, he was more than two hundred years ahead of her on the evolutionary scale. It was a pity she was so intriguing. And so primitively attractive. But he was a scientist, and he had already calculated that any kind of involvement with her would shoot his equations to hell.

Still, she was right about one thing, he decided. They were stuck with each other. The whole damn mountain was practically empty but for the two of them. The way the snow was falling, it was painfully obvious that they would be in each other's way for days. However irritating it might be, for the time being, he needed her.

He had to get around her, or through her, to get to his brother. Whatever it took, he would get to Cal.

Turning, he made a long, slow study of the kitchen. The first thing to be faced was that the cabin was too small for them to avoid each other. He could go back to his ship, but he preferred being here, recording first-hand observations. It would be easier to fight whatever attraction Cal felt for this time and place if he understood it. And his innate curiosity would never be satisfied on the ship.

So he would stay. And if that made the pretty Sunbeam uncomfortable, so much the better.

His own discomfort—and the kiss had caused him plenty—would just have to be dealt with. He was, after all, superior.

Feeling more calm, he went back to the table to re-assemble the toaster.

As he worked, he could hear the ceiling creak and groan above his head. He smiled to himself when he realized that she was pacing on the second floor. He bothered her. And that was just fine. Maybe she would keep her distance—or at least stop daring him to do something they would both regret.

It was illogical to desire someone he didn't even like. To fantasize about someone he could barely tolerate. To ache for someone who annoyed him so consistently.

When the screwdriver slipped and mashed his thumb, he cursed her again.

He wasn't going to get away with it. She paced from wall to wall, from window to door, trying to work off steam. The nerve of the man, to grab her as if she were some mindless bimbo, then reject her just as callously. Did he think, did he really think, he could vent his... his sexual frustrations on her without compunction?

She had news for him.

No one, absolutely no one, treated her in that manner and lived to tell the tale. She'd been taking care of herself for too long. Men might pressure. She pushed them aside. They might seduce. She resisted, effort-lessly. They might beg. She—

Her smile bloomed beautifully at the image of Jacob

Hornblower begging. Oh, that would be a triumph, she thought. The enigmatic Dr. Hornblower on his knees, at her feet.

With a sigh, she began pacing again. It was a shame, a damn shame, that her standards didn't permit teasing or clichéd feminine ploys. No matter how much of a jerk he was, she had her ethics.

She was a modern woman, one who stood on her own, with or without a man. One who thought her own thoughts and fought her own fights. She was no Delilah to use sex as a weapon. But she wished, and how she wished, that once, just this once, she could ignore those ingrained principles and seduce him into a pitiful puddle of pleading.

He'd used sex, she thought, kicking a shoe out of her path. And wasn't that just like a man? They liked to claim that it was women who lured and teased and taunted. Incensed, she gave the hapless shoe a second, vicious kick. Men, the entire bloody species, preferred to play the innocent bystander entrapped by the femme fatale. Hah!

If anyone dared to call Sunny Stone a femme fatale she'd punch him right in the face.

He'd forced himself on *her*. Well, her stiff-necked honesty pushed her to admit that he hadn't used force for more than a fraction of a second—if at all. Before he'd kissed her senseless.

She hated that. The fact that she'd melted like some weak-kneed romantic heroine. She'd kissed him back, too. What was the word? Wantonly. It made her wince. One lousy kiss and she'd been plastered all over him. So, she owed him for that, as well.

The best way to pay him back, she realized, was to shoot straight for the ego. As far as she could tell, that was the biggest target a man offered a woman. Hiding in her room would only make him think he—and what had happened between them—mattered to her. So she would go about her business and act as though nothing had happened.

He was still in the kitchen when she came down. Sunny turned on the stereo and adjusted the volume. If it was loud enough, conversation would be difficult, if not impossible. After adding a log to the fire, she settled on the sofa with her books. Over an hour passed before he came out and went upstairs. She studiously ignored him.

More from boredom than from appetite, she went into the kitchen and fixed herself an enormous sandwich. Under other circumstances she would have offered to make one for her guest. But the idea of him going hungry just made her own meal that much more palatable.

Content, she bundled into coat and boots to go outside and fill the bird feeder. The short trip brought home to her the fact that her unwelcome company would be in her way for several days. The snow was blinding, falling in swirling sheets that covered her tracks almost as quickly as she made them. There was wind behind it, a nasty wind that raced keening through the trees and sent the pines roaring.

With snow up to the tops of her boots, she lugged the bag of feed back to the shed. Catching her breath, she let the storm blow around her. She could see nothing but the power of it, the anger of it. It was magnificent.

Annoyance faded. All dark thoughts vanished. As she stood with the wind battering her, the snow slapping wet on her cheeks, she felt the excitement and the peace that she rarely felt elsewhere.

Though she never stayed in the mountains long, though she always became restless and went off in search of noise and crowds, there was no place she would rather be in a storm. Winter snow or summer thunder. It was here, alone, that the force, the energy, the mystery, could be appreciated.

A city covered with snow would soon dig itself out. But the mountains were patient. They would wait for sun and time. As she stood with the wind wrapped around her like a wild, relentless lover she wished she could take some piece of this with her wherever she went.

From the window he watched her. She stood like

some kind of winter goddess in the whirling snow. Hatless, her coat flapping open, she remained still, heedless, as the snow covered her hair. And she was smiling. Cold colored her cheeks. She seemed more than beautiful now. She seemed untouchable. And invincible.

He wondered as he looked down on her why he wanted her more at that moment than he had when she had been hot and passionate in his arms.

Then she looked up, as if she knew he was watching. Through the blowing curtain of snow, their eyes met. His hands balled into fists, fists identical to the one that clenched in his gut. She was no longer smiling. Despite the distance, he felt the power ricochet back to him, buckling his knees.

If he could have reached out for her then, he would have taken her, regardless of the consequences. In that one look, past, present and future merged into one. He saw his destiny.

Then she shifted, shaking the snow from her hair, and the spell shattered. He told himself she was only a woman, a foolish one, walking in a storm. She would have no lasting effect on him.

But it was a long time after he heard her come inside before he went downstairs again.

She was sleeping on the sofa, books piled at her feet and on the floor. One of the exquisite throws was tossed over her. Despite the volume of the stereo, she slept deeply. Nearby, the fire blazed.

She didn't look invincible now, Jacob decided. She looked disconcertingly serene. He supposed it was foolish to notice how long her lashes were as they shadowed her cheeks. How soft her mouth was when relaxed in sleep. How her hair, mussed from the wind, shone in the firelight.

They were only physical attributes, and in his time physical appearance could be altered simply and safely. It made life more pleasant, certainly, to look at a beautiful woman. But it was superficial. Totally superficial. Still, he looked for a long time.

Sunny woke like a shot when the music cut off. The abrupt silence had her leaping out of sleep with eyes wide and curses on her tongue. Disoriented and irritable, as she always was upon waking, she stared around the darkened room. The fire had burned down to a soft glow and shed little light. Though she didn't think she had slept long, night had fallen. And so, she realized, had a power line.

With a sigh, she pushed herself from the sofa and groped her way across the room looking for matches. With a candle in one hand and a pack of matches in the other, she turned and walked into Jacob.

At her quick squeal, he brought his hands to her arms, both to steady and to reassure. "It's only me."

"I know who it is," she snapped, infuriated that she'd jolted. "What are you doing?"

"Before or after the lights went out?"

She could see him well enough, silhouetted by the firelight, to make out the smile. "It's the storm."

"What about it?" The muscles in her arms were tensed. He had to resist the urge to slip his hands up the sleeves of her sweater and soothe them and stroke her skin.

"It knocked out the power."

He hadn't let her go. He'd told himself to, but his hands hadn't listened. "Would you like me to fix it?"

Her laugh was quick and a bit unsteady. She wished she could blame the power failure for her nerves, but she'd never been afraid of the dark. Until now. "It's a little more complicated than a toaster. The power company will get to it when they can."

He was sure he could jury-rig something, but he didn't mind the dark. "All right."

All right, she thought, letting out a long breath. In the meantime, she was alone with him. Added to the fact that she wasn't sure about his mental balance was the very real problem of being attracted to him. One thing at a time, she told herself, and took a deliberate step back.

"We have plenty of candles." To prove it, she lit the one she held in her hand. It helped her confidence when she saw the flame hold steady. "And plenty of wood. If you'll put a couple of logs on the fire, I'll deal with getting us more light."

He watched the way the small flame flickered in her eyes. She was nervous, he realized, and wished that didn't make her even more seductive. "Sure."

Sunny gathered every candle she could put her hands on. Too late she realized that one or two would have seemed rustic. The dozen she had scattered through the room only added an impossibly romantic atmosphere. Stuffing the matches in her pocket, she reminded herself that she wasn't affected by things like atmosphere.

"You wouldn't know what time it is, would you?" she asked him.

"Not exactly. Around six."

She sat on the arm of the sofa nearest the fire. "I slept longer than I thought." Now she was going to have to make the best of a bad situation. "So, did you entertain yourself this afternoon?"

"I fixed the faucet." It had taken more time and given him more trouble than he'd anticipated, but he'd managed.

"You're a regular Harry Homemaker, aren't you?" Because it sounded sarcastic, she smiled. They really did only have each other at this point, and alienating him wouldn't be wise. "I could fix some sandwiches." She rose, willing to be gracious if it kept her busy. "Want a beer?"

"Yeah. Thanks."

Sunny took two of the candles into the kitchen and nearly relaxed before she realized he'd followed her in. "I can manage this by myself." She opened the refrigerator and swore when she remembered that the light wouldn't come on. Saying nothing, Jacob handed her a candle. She shoved two beers at him.

He remembered how she had dealt with the bottles that morning, and he was delighted when he found the same tool and popped the tops.

"Switch on the radio, will you?"

"What?"

"The radio," she repeated. "On the windowsill. We might get a weather report."

He found a small plastic box. He was grinning at it as he found the dial and turned on static.

"Mess with the tuner," she advised him.

He was contemplating *borrowing* it and taking it back home. "Mess with it?"

"You know…fool with it. See if you can come up with a station."

He stared at the little portable for a moment, wondering how one fooled an inanimate object. Making sure Sunny's back was to him, he took the radio off the windowsill and shook it. Because that seemed stupid, he began to turn dials. The static faded in and out.

"Mustard or mayo?"

"What?"

"On your sandwich," she said, striving for patience. "Do you want mustard or mayo?"

"It doesn't matter. Whatever you're having." He found some tinny music that was almost audible. How did people tolerate such unreliable equipment? he wondered. At home he had a portable unit that could give him the weather in Paris, a play-by-play of a ball game, a traffic report from Mars and a passable cup of coffee. Simultaneously. This antique child's toy wasn't coming up with anything more than what sounded like a banjo playing in a wind tunnel.

"Let me try." Setting the sandwiches aside, Sunny snatched the radio from him. In moments there was a blast of music. "It's temperamental," she explained.

"It's a machine," he reminded her, miffed.

"A temperamental one." Satisfied, she set it back on the counter, then carried her sandwich and her beer to the table. "Weather report's not much use anyway." She applied herself to the sandwich. "I already know it's snowing."

Jacob picked up one of the potato chips she had piled beside the bread. "More to the point is to know when it's going to stop."

"Speculation." She shrugged as he joined her. "No matter how many satellites they put up there, it's still guesswork."

He opened his mouth to contradict her but thought better of it and bit into his sandwich instead. "Does it bother you?"

"What?"

"Being…" What phrase would she use? "Being cut off."

"Not really—at least not for a day or two. After that I start to go crazy." She winced, wondering if that was the best choice of words. "How about you?"

"I don't like being closed in," he said simply. He had to smile when he heard the light tap of her foot on the floor. He was making her nervous again. He took an experimental swig of beer. "This is good." He glanced around when a voice broke into the music to announce the weather. The cheerful, painfully breezy announcer carried on for several moments before getting to the mountains.

"And you people way up in the Klamath might as well snuggle up. Hope you've got your main squeeze with you, 'cause it looks like you're in for a big one. The white stuff's going to keep right on falling through tomorrow night. Expect about three feet, you hardy souls, with winds gusting up to thirty miles an hour. *Brrr!* Temperatures down to fifteen tonight, not counting old Mr. Wind Chill. Bundle up, baby, and let *looove* keep you warm."

"Not very scientific," Jacob murmured.

Sunny made a rude noise and scowled at the radio. "However it's presented, it means the same thing. I'd better bring in some more wood."

"I'll get it."

"I don't need—"

"You made the sandwiches," he pointed out, sipping more beer. "I'll get the wood when we're finished."

"Fine." She didn't want him to do her any favors. She ate in silence for a time, watching him. "You'd have been better off to wait until spring."

"For what?"

"To come to see Cal."

He took another bite of his sandwich. He wasn't sure what it was, but it was terrific. "Apparently. Actually, I'd planned to be here…sooner." Almost a year sooner. "But it didn't work out."

"It's a shame your parents couldn't come with you… you know, to visit."

She saw something in his eyes then. Regret, frustration, anger? She couldn't be sure. "It wasn't possible."

She refused, absolutely, to feel sorry for him. "My parents couldn't stand not seeing Libby or me for so long."

The disapproval in her voice rubbed an already raw

wound. "You have no conception of how the separation from Cal has affected my family."

"Sorry." But she moved her shoulders to show that she wasn't. "I'd just think if they were anxious to see him they'd have made the effort to do so."

"The choice was his." He pushed back from the table. "I'll get the wood."

Touchy, touchy, she thought as he started toward the door. "Hey."

He rounded on her, ready to fight. "What?"

"You can't go out without a coat. It's freezing."

"I don't have one with me."

"Are all scientists so softheaded?" she muttered. Rising, she went into a long cupboard. "I can't think of anything so stupid as to come into the mountains in January without a coat."

Jacob took a deep breath and then said calmly, "If you keep calling me stupid, I'm going to have to hit you."

She gave him a bland look. "I'm shaking. Here." She tossed him a worn pea coat. "Put that on. The last thing I want is to have to treat you for frostbite." As an afterthought, she threw him a pair of gloves and a dark stocking cap. "You do have winters in Philadelphia, don't you?"

His teeth gritted, Jacob struggled into the coat. "It

wasn't cold when I left home." He dragged the hat down over his ears.

"Oh, well, that certainly explains it." She gave a snort of laughter when he slammed the door behind him. He wasn't really crazy, she thought. A little dim, maybe, and so much fun to aggravate. And if she aggravated him enough, Sunny mused, she might just get some more information out of him.

She heard him cursing and didn't bother to muffle a laugh. Unless she missed her guess, he'd just dropped at least one log on his foot. Perhaps she should have offered him a flashlight, but...he deserved it.

Wiping the grin from her face, she went to the door to open it for him. He was already coated with snow. It was even clinging to his eyebrows, giving him a fiercely surprised expression. She bit down hard on her tongue and let him stomp across the kitchen, his arms loaded with wood. At the sound of logs crashing into the box, she cleared her throat, then calmly picked up her beer and his before joining him in the living room.

"I'll get the next load," she told him solicitously.

"You bet you will." His foot was throbbing, his fingers were numb, and his temper was already lost. "How does anybody live like this?"

"Like what?" she asked innocently.

"Here." He was at his wit's end. He threw out his arms in a gesture that encompassed not only the cabin but also the world at large. "You have no power, no conveniences, no decent transportation, no nothing. If you want heat, you have to burn wood. Wood, for God's sake! If you want light, you have to rely on unstable electricity. As for communication, it's a joke. A bad one."

Sunny was a city girl at heart, but nobody insulted her family home. Her chin came up. "Listen, pal, if I hadn't taken you in you'd be up in the woods freezing like a Popsicle and no one would have found you until the spring thaw. So watch it."

Overly sensitive, he decided, lifting a brow. "You can't tell me that you actually like it here."

Her hands fisted and landed on her hips. "I like it here just fine. If you don't, we've got two doors. Take your pick."

His little excursion to the woodpile had convinced him that he didn't care to brave the elements. Neither did he care to swallow his pride. He stood for a moment, considering his choices. Without a word, he picked up his beer, sat and drank.

Since Sunny considered it a victory, she joined him. But she wasn't ready to give him a break. "You're awfully finicky for a guy who pops up on the doorstep without so much as a toothbrush."

"Excuse me?"

"I said you're awfully—"

"How do you know I don't have a toothbrush?" He'd read about them. Now, with fire glinting in his eyes, he turned to her.

"It's an expression," Sunny said, evading his question. "I simply meant that I wouldn't think that a man who travels with one change of clothes should be complaining about the accommodations."

"How would you know what I've got—unless you've been going through my things?"

"You haven't got any things," Sunny muttered, knowing that once again she'd opened her mouth before she'd fine-tuned her brain. She started to rise, but he clamped a hand on her shoulder. "Look, I only went through your bag to see—just to see, that's all." She turned, deciding a level look was the best defense. "How could I be sure you were who you said you were and not some maniac?"

He kept his grip painfully firm. "And are you sure now?" He caught the quick flicker in her eyes and decided to exploit it. "There wasn't anything in my bag to tell you one way or the other. Was there?"

"Maybe not." She tried to shrug his hand off. When it remained, she balled one of her own into a fist and waited.

"So, for all you know, I am a maniac." He leaned closer, until his face was an inch from hers, until her eyes saw only his eyes, until his breath mingled with her breath. "And there are all kinds of maniacs, aren't there, Sunny?"

"Yes." She had trouble getting the word past her lips. It wasn't fear. She wished it were. It was something much more complicated, much more dangerous, than fear. For a moment, with the firelight flickering beside them, the candles wavering, the wind beating soft fists on the window, she didn't care who he was. All that mattered was that he was going to kiss her. And more.

The fact that he would do more was in his eyes. The image of rolling on the floor with him sprang into her mind. A wild, willful tangle of bodies, a free, frantic burst of passion. It would be that way with him. The first time, and every time. Raging rivers, quaking earth, exploding planets. Such would love be with him.

And after the first time there would be no turning back. She was certain, as she had never been certain of anything, that if there was a first time, she would want him, she would crave him, as long as there was breath in her body.

His lips brushed hers. It could hardly be called a kiss, yet the potency of it sent shock waves streaking through her system. And had warning bells screaming in her head. She did the only thing a sensible woman could do under the circumstances. She drove her clenched hand into his stomach.

His breath pushed out in a huff of pained surprise. As

he doubled over, nearly falling in her lap, she slipped to one side and sprang to her feet. She was braced and ready for his next move.

"You're the maniac," he managed after he'd wheezed some air into his lungs. "I have never in my life met anyone like you."

"Thanks." She was nibbling on her lip again, but she let her tensed arms drop to her sides. "You deserved that, J.T." She held her ground as he slowly lifted his head and sent her a long, killing look. "You were trying to intimidate me."

It had started out that way, he was forced to admit. But in the end, when he had leaned toward her, smelled her hair, felt the soft silk of her lips, it had had nothing to do with intimidation and everything to do with seduction. His. "It wouldn't be hard," he said after a moment, "to learn to detest you."

"No, I guess not." Because he was taking it better than she'd anticipated, she smiled at him. "I tell you what—since we are family, so to speak... I do believe you, by the way. That you're Cal's brother, I mean."

"Thanks." Finally he managed to straighten up. "Thanks a lot."

"Don't mention it. As I was saying, since we're sort of family, why don't we call a truce? It's like this—if the weather keeps up, we're going to be trapped here together for several days."

"Now who's trying to intimidate whom?"

She laughed then and decided to be friendly. "Just laying my cards on the table. If we keep throwing punches at each other, we're only going to get bruised. I figure it's not worth it."

He had to think about that, and think hard. "I wouldn't mind going for two out of three."

"You're a tough nut, J.T."

Since he didn't know what to make of that description, he kept silent.

"I still vote for the truce, at least until the snow stops. I don't hit you anymore and you don't try to kiss me again. Deal?"

He liked the part about her not hitting him anymore. And he'd already decided he wouldn't *try* to kiss her again. He would damn well *do* it, whenever he chose to. He nodded. "Deal."

"Excellent. We'll celebrate the truce with another beer and some popcorn. We've got an old popper in the kitchen. We can make it over the fire."

"Sunny." She paused, candle in hand, in the doorway. He couldn't help but resent the way the flickering light flattered her. "I'm still not sure I like you."

"That's okay." She smiled. "I'm not sure I like you, either."

Chapter 5

She might have called it rustic. He might have called it primitive. But there was something soothing, peaceful and calming about popping corn over an open fire.

She seemed to have the hang of it, he thought, as she shook the long-handled box over the flames. The scent was enough to make his mouth water as the kernels began to pop and batter the screened metal lid. Though he could have explained scientifically how the hard seeds exploded into fluffy white pieces, it was more fun just to watch.

"We'd always make popcorn this way here," she murmured, watching the flames. "Even in the summer, when we were sweltering, Mom or Dad would build a fire and we'd fight over who got to hold the popper." Her lips curved at the memory.

"You were happy here."

"Sure. I probably would have gone on being happy here, but I discovered the world. What do you think of the world, J.T.?"

"Which one?"

With a laugh, she gave the popper an extra shake. "I should have known better than to ask an astro-whatever. Your mind's probably in space half the time."

"At least."

She sat cross-legged on the floor, the firelight glowing on her face and hair. That face, he thought, with its exquisite bones and angles, was perfectly relaxed. She was obviously taking the truce seriously, rambling on, as friendly as a longtime friend, about whatever came to mind.

He sipped his beer and listened, though he knew next to nothing about the movies and music she spoke of. Or the books. Some of the titles were vaguely familiar, but he had spent very little of his time reading fiction.

He'd touched on some twentieth-century entertainment in his research, but not enough to make him an expert in the areas Sunny seemed so well versed in.

"You don't like movies?" she asked at length.

"I didn't say that."

"You haven't seen any of the flicks I've mentioned that have been popular in the last eighteen months."

He wondered what she'd say if he told her that the

last video he'd seen had been produced in 2250. "It's just that I've been busy in the lab for quite a while."

She felt a tug of sympathy for him. Sunny didn't mind working, and working hard, but she expected plenty of time for fun. "Don't they ever give you a break?"

"Who?"

"The people you work for." She switched hands and continued to shake the popper.

That made him smile a little, since for the past five years he had been in the position of calling his own shots and hiring his own people. "It's more a matter of me being obsessed with the project I've been working on."

"Which is?"

He waited a beat, then decided that the truth couldn't hurt. In fact, he wanted to see her reaction. "Time travel."

She laughed, but then she saw his face and cleared her throat. "You're not joking."

"No." He glanced at the popper. "I think you're burning it."

"Oh." She jerked it out of the flames and set it down on the hearth. "You really mean time travel, like H. G. Wells?"

"Not precisely." He stretched out his legs so that the fire warmed the soles of his feet. "Time and space are relative—in simple terms. It's a matter of finding the proper equations and implementing them."

"Sure. E equals MC squared, but really, J.T., bopping around through time?" She shook her head, obviously amused. "Like Mr. Peabody and Sherman in the Wayback machine."

"Who?"

"You obviously had a deprived childhood. It's a cartoon, you know? And this dog scientist—"

He held up a hand, his eyes narrowed to green slits. "A dog was a scientist?"

"In the cartoon," she said patiently. "And he had this boy, Sherman. Never mind," she added when she saw his expression. "It's just that they would set the dates on this big machine."

"The Wayback."

"Exactly. Then they would travel back, like to Nero's Rome or Arthur's Britain."

"Fascinating."

"Entertaining. It was a cartoon, J.T. You can't really believe it."

He sent her a slow, enigmatic smile. "Do you only believe what you can see?"

"No." She frowned, using a hot pad to remove the lid from the popper. "I guess not." Then she laughed and sampled the popcorn. "Maybe I do. I'm a realist. We really needed one in the family."

"Even a realist has to accept certain possibilities."

"I suppose." She took another handful and decided to get into the spirit of things. "Okay. So, we're in Mr. Peabody's Wayback machine. Where would you go—or when, I suppose I should say? When would you go, if you really could?"

He looked at her, sitting in the firelight, laughter still in her eyes. "The possibilities are endless. What about you?"

"I wonder." She held the beer loosely in her hand as she considered. "I imagine Libby would have a dozen places to go back to. The Aztecs, the Incas, the Mayans. Dad would probably want to see Tombstone or Dodge City. And my mother…well, she'd go where my father went, to keep an eye on him."

He dipped into the popcorn. "I asked about you."

"I'd go forward. I'd want to see what was coming."

He didn't speak, only stared into the fire.

"A hundred, maybe two hundred, years in the future. After all, you can read history books and get a pretty good idea of what things were like before. But after… It seems to me it would be much more exciting to see just what we've made out of things." The idea made her laugh up at him. "Do they actually pay you to work on stuff like that? I mean, wouldn't it make more sense to figure out how to travel across town in, say, Manhattan in under forty minutes during rush hour?"

"I'm free to choose my own projects."

"Must be nice." She was mellow now, relaxed and happy enough with his company. "It seems I've spent most of my life trying to figure out what I wanted to do. I'm a terrible employee," she admitted with a sigh. "It's something about rules and authority. I'm argumentative."

"Really?"

She didn't mind his grin. "Really. But I'm so often right, you see, that it's really hard to admit when I'm wrong. Sometimes I wish I was more…flexible."

"Why? The world's full of people who give in."

"Maybe they're happier," she murmured. "It's a shame the word *compromise* is so hard to swallow. You don't like to be wrong, either."

"I make sure I'm not."

She laughed and stretched out on the rug. "Maybe I do like you. We're going to have to tend this fire all night unless we want to freeze. We'll take shifts." She yawned and pillowed her head over her hands. "Wake me up in a couple of hours and I'll take over."

When he was certain she was asleep, Jacob covered her with the colorful blanket, then left her by the fire. Upstairs, it took him less than ten minutes to make some adjustments to the desktop computer and tie it in so that it would run off his mini unit. The mini didn't have the memory banks of his ship model, but it would be enough to make his report and answer the few questions he had.

"Engage, computer."

A quiet, neutral voice answered him. *Engaged*.

"Report. Hornblower, Jacob. Current date is January 20th. A winter storm has caused me to remain in the cabin. The structure runs off electric power, typically unreliable in this era. Apparently the power is transmitted through overhead lines that are vulnerable during storms. At approximately 1800 hours, the power was cut off. Estimated time of repair?"

Working... Incomplete data.

"I was afraid of that." He paused for a moment, thinking. "Sunbeam Stone is resourceful. Candles—wax candles—are used for light. Wood is burned for heat. It is, of course, insufficient, and only accommodates a small area. It is, however..." He searched for a word. "...pleasant. It creates a certain soothing ambiance." Annoyed, he cut himself off. He didn't want to think of the way she had looked in the firelight. "As reported earlier, Stone is a difficult and aggressive female, prone to bursts of temper. She is also disarmingly generous, sporadically friendly and—" The word *desirable* was on the tip of his tongue. Jacob bit it. "Intriguing," he decided. "Further study is necessary. However, I do not believe she is an average woman of this time." He paused again, drumming his fingers on the desk. "Computer, what are the typical attitudes of women toward mating in this era?"

Working.

As soon as he had asked, Jacob opened his mouth to disengage. But the computer was quick.

Most typically physical attraction, sometimes referred to as chemistry, is required. Emotional attachment, ranging from affection to love, is preferred by 97.6 percent of females. Single encounters, often called one-night stands, were no longer fashionable in this part of the twentieth century. Subjects preferred commitment from sexual partners. Romance was widely accepted and desired.

"Define 'romance.'"

Working... To influence by personal attention, flattery or gifts. Also synonymous with love, love affair, an attachment between male and female. Typified by the atmosphere of dim lighting, quiet music, flowers. Accepted romantic gestures include—

"That's enough." Jacob rubbed his hands over his face and wondered if he was going crazy. He had no business wasting time asking the computer such unscientific questions. He had less business contemplating a totally unscientific relationship with Sunny Stone.

He had only two purposes for being where he was. The first and most important was to find his brother. The second was to gather as much data as possible about this era. Sunny Stone was data, and she couldn't be anything else.

But he wanted her. It was unscientific, but it was very real. It was also illogical. How could he want to be with a woman who annoyed him as much as she amused him? Why should he care about a woman he had so little in common with? Centuries separated them. Her world, while fascinating in a clinical sense, frustrated the hell out of him. *She* frustrated the hell out of him.

The best thing to do was to get back to his ship, program his computers and go home. If it weren't for Cal, he would do so. He wanted to think it was only Cal that stopped him.

Meticulously, he disengaged the computer and pocketed his mini. When he returned downstairs, she was still sleeping. Moving quietly, he put another log on the fire, then sat on the floor beside her.

Hours passed, but he didn't bother to wake her. He was used to functioning on little or no sleep. For more than a year his average workday had run eighteen hours. The closer he had come to the final equations for time travel, the more he had pushed. And he had succeeded, he thought as he watched the flames eat the wood. He was here. Of course, even with his meticulous computations, he had come several months too late.

Cal was married, of all things. And if Sunny was to be believed, he was happy and settled. It would be that much more difficult for Jacob to make him see reason. But he would make him see it.

He had to see it, Jacob told himself. It was as clear as glass. A man belonged in his own time. There were reasons, purposes. Beyond what science could do, there was a pattern. If a man chose to break that pattern, the ripple effects on the rest of the universe couldn't be calculated.

So he would take his brother back to where they both belonged. And Cal would soon forget the woman called Libby. Just as Jacob was determined to forget Sunbeam Stone.

She stirred then, with a soft, sighing sound that tingled along his skin. Despite his better judgment, he looked down and watched her wake.

Her lashes fluttered open and closed, as exotic as butterfly wings in the shadowed light. Her eyes, dazed with sleep, were huge and dark. She didn't see him, but stared blindly into the flickering flame as she slowly stretched her long, lean body, muscle by muscle. The bulky purple sweater shifted over her curves.

His mouth went dry. His heartbeat accelerated. He would have cursed her, but he lacked the strength. At that moment she was so outrageously beautiful that he could only sit, tensed, and pray for sanity.

She let out a little moan. He winced. She shifted onto her back, lifting her arms over her head, then up to the ceiling. For the first time in his life he actively wished for a drink.

At last she turned her head and focused on him. "Why didn't you wake me?"

Her voice was low, throaty. Jacob was certain he could feel his blood drain to the soles of his feet. "I—" It was ridiculous, but he could barely speak. "I wasn't tired."

"That's not the point." She sat up and said crankily, "We're in this together, so—"

He didn't think. Later, when he had time to analyze, he would tell himself it was reflex—the same involuntary reflex that makes a man swallow when water is poured down his throat. It was not deliberate. It was not planned. It was certainly not wise.

He pulled her against him, dragging one hand through her hair before closing his mouth over hers. She bucked, both surprise and anger giving her strength. But he only tightened his hold. It was desperation this time, a sensation he could not remember ever having felt for a woman. It was taste her or die.

She struggled to cling to her anger as dozens of sensations fought for control of her. Delight, desire, delirium. She tried to curse him, but managed only a moan of pleasure. Then her hands were in his hair, clenching, and her heart was pounding. In one quick movement he drew her onto his lap and drove her beyond.

His breath was ragged, as was hers. His mouth frantic, his hands quick. Left without choice, she answered, as insistent, as insatiable, as he. A log broke apart, sparks flew to dance on stone. The wind gusted, pushing a puff of smoke into the room. She heard only the urgent groan that slipped from his mouth into hers.

Was this what she had been searching for? The excitement, the challenge, the glory? Heedlessly she gave herself to it, let the power swamp her.

The taste of her seemed to explode inside him, over and over. Hot, pungent, lusty. It wasn't enough. The more he took, the more he needed. Dragging her head back, he found her throat, the long, slender line of it enticing him, the warm, seductive flavor of it bewitching him. He skimmed his lips over the curve of it, letting his tongue and his teeth toy with her skin. It was still not enough.

As the firelight played over her face, he slipped his hands under the bulky sweater to find her. Her skin brought him images of rose petals, of heated satin. There was trembling as his hand closed over her breast. From her, from him.

With his eyes on hers, and shadows dancing between them, he lowered his mouth once more.

It was like sinking into a dream. Not a soft, misty one, but one full of sound and color. And, as he sank deeper, she wrapped herself around him. Her hands searched as his did, under his sweater, along the ridges of muscles.

As his lips began to roam over her face, she let her eyes close once again. And her heart, always so strong and valiant, was lost.

Love poured into her like a revelation. It left her gasping and clinging. It had her lips heating against his, her body liquefying. Her hands, always capable, slid helplessly down his arms.

Helplessly.

It was that which had her stiffening against him, pulling back, resisting. This couldn't be love. It was absurd, and dangerous, to think it could be.

"Jacob, stop."

"Stop?" He closed his teeth, none too gently, over her chin.

"Yes. Stop."

He could feel the change, the frustrating withdrawal of her while his body was still humming. "Why?"

"Because I..."

In a calculated movement, he skimmed his fingers down her spine, playing them over vulnerable nerves. He watched as her eyes glazed and her head fell back, limp. "I want you, Sunny. And you want me."

"Yes." What was he doing to her? She lifted a hand in protest, then dropped it weakly and let it rest against his chest. "No. Don't do that."

"Do what?"

"Whatever you're doing."

She was trembling now, shuddering. Completely vulnerable. He cursed himself. It was a shock to realize that when she was defenseless he was hampered by ethics. "Fine." He grasped her hips and set her back on the floor.

Shaken, she hugged her knees to her chest. She felt as though she'd been plucked out of a furnace and tossed into ice. "This shouldn't be happening. And it certainly shouldn't be happening so fast."

"It is happening," he told her. "And it's foolish to pretend otherwise."

She glanced up as he rose to feed the fire. The heat still pumped out of the logs. A few of the candles they had left lit were guttering out. Outside the window there was a lessening of the darkness, so dawn had to be breaking beyond the storm. The wind still whooshed at the windows.

She had forgotten all that. All that and more. When she had been in his arms there had been no storm except the one raging inside her. There had been no fire but her own passions. The one promise she had made herself, never to lose control over a man, had been broken.

"It's easy for you, isn't it?" she said, with a bitterness that surprised her.

He looked back to study her. No, it wasn't easy for him. It should be, but it wasn't. And he was baffled by it. "Why should it be complicated?" The question was as much for himself as for her.

"I don't make love with strangers." She sprang to her feet with a fierce wish for coffee and solitude. Leaving him, she marched into the kitchen and plucked a soft drink from the refrigerator. She'd take her caffeine cold.

He waited a moment, going over what the computer had told him. The physical attraction was certainly there. And, as much as he detested the idea, his emotions were involved. It did no good to be angry. She was obviously reacting normally, given the situation. And it was he who was out of step. It was a sobering thought, but one that had to be faced.

But he still wanted her. And now he intended to pursue her. Logically, his success factor would increase if he pursued her in a manner she would expect from a typical twentieth-century man.

Jacob blew out a long breath. He didn't know precisely what that might entail, but he thought he understood the first step. It was doubtful that much had changed in any millennium.

When he walked into the kitchen, she was staring out the window at the monotonously falling snow. "Sunny." Oh, it went against the grain. "I apologize."

"I don't want your apology."

Jacob cast his eyes at the ceiling and prayed for patience. "What do you want?"

"Nothing." It amazed her that she was on the brink of tears. She never cried. She hated it, considered it a weak, embarrassing experience. Sunny always preferred a screaming rage to tears. But she felt tears burning behind her eyes now and stubbornly fought them back. "Just forget it."

"Forget what happened, or forget the fact that I'm attracted to you?"

"Either or both." She turned then. Though her eyes were dry, they were overbright, and they made him acutely uncomfortable. "It doesn't matter."

"Obviously it does." It shouldn't, but there seemed to be nothing he could do to change it. If she kept looking at him like that, he would have to touch her again. In self-defense he stuffed his hands in his pockets. "Maybe we've gotten our codes mixed."

Hurt was temporarily blocked by bafflement. "I don't—do you mean we got our signals crossed?"

"I suppose."

Tired all over again, she dragged a hand through her hair. "I doubt it. We'll just call it a temporary lapse."

"And do what?"

She wished she knew. "Look, J.T., we're both adults. All we have to do is act like it."

"I thought we were." He tried a smile. "I'm sorry I upset you."

"It wasn't completely your fault." She managed to smile back at him. "Circumstances. We're alone here, the power's out. Candle and firelight." She shrugged and felt miserable. "Anybody could get carried away."

"If you say so." He took a step forward. She took a step back. The pursuit, Jacob decided, was going to require strategy. "But I am attracted to you, even without candlelight."

She started to speak, discovered she didn't know what she wanted to say and dragged her hands through her hair again. "You should get some sleep. I'm going for more wood."

"All right. Sunbeam?"

She turned back, shooting him a look of amusement and exasperation at his use of her full name.

"I enjoyed kissing you," he told her. "Very much."

Muttering under her breath, she bundled into her coat and escaped outside.

The day passed slowly. Sunny might have wished he would sleep longer, but it hardly mattered. Awake or asleep, he was there. As long as he was, he intruded. At times, though she tried to bury herself in her books, she was so painfully aware of him that she nearly groaned.

He read—voraciously, Sunny thought—novel after

novel from the bookshelf. Activity was almost completely confined to the living room and the warmth of the fire, which they took turns feeding.

At lunchtime they fell back on cold sandwiches, though she did manage to boil water over the fire for tea. They spoke to each other only when it was impossible not to.

By evening they were both wildly restless, edgy from confinement and from the fact that both of them wondered what the day would have been like if they had spent it under a blanket, together, rather than at opposite ends of the room.

He paced to one window. She paced to another. She poked at the fire. He leafed through yet another book. She went for a bag of cookies. He went for fresh candles.

"Have you ever read this?"

Sunny glanced over. It was the first word they had spoken to each other in an hour. "What?"

"Jane Eyre."

"Oh, sure." It was a relief to have a conversation again. She handed him the bag of cookies as a peace offering.

"What did you think of it?"

"I always like reading about the mannerisms of an earlier century. They were so stringent and puritanical back then, with all that passion boiling underneath the civilized veneer."

He had to smile. "Do you think so?"

"Sure. And of course it's beautifully written, and wonderfully romantic." She sat with her legs hooked over the arm of a chair, her eyes a little sleepy and her scent—damn her—everywhere. "The plain, penniless girl capturing the heart of the bold, brooding hero."

He gave her a puzzled look. "That's romantic?"

"Of course. Then there's windswept moors and painful tragedy, sacrifice. They did a terrific production of it on PBS a few years ago. Did you see it?"

"No." He set the book aside, still puzzled. "My mother has a copy at home. She loves to read novels."

"That's probably because she needs to relax after being in court all day."

"Probably."

"What does your father do?"

"This and that." Suddenly his family seemed incredibly far away. "He likes to garden."

"So does mine. Herbs, naturally." She gestured toward her empty teacup. "But he putters around with flowers, too. When we were little he grew vegetables right outside the kitchen. It's practically all we ate, which is why I avoid them now."

He tried to imagine it and simply couldn't. "What was it like growing up here?"

"It seemed natural." She rose idly to poke at the fire, then sat on the couch beside him, forgetting for a moment how restless the storm was making her. "I guess I thought everyone lived like we did, until we went to the city and I saw the lights, the crowds, the buildings. For me, it was as if someone had broken open a kaleidoscope and handed me all the colors. We would always come back here, and that was fine." With a half yawn, she sank back into the cushions. "But I always wanted to get back to all that noise. Nothing changes much here, and that's nice, because you can always depend on it. But there's always something new in the city. I guess I like progress."

"But you're here now."

"A self-imposed penance, in a way."

"For what?"

She moved her shoulders. "It's a long story. What about you? Are you a city boy yearning for the peace of the country?"

He glanced deliberately out the window. "No."

She laughed and patted his hand. "So here we are, two city dwellers stuck in the wilds of the Northwest. Want to play cards?"

His mood brightened instantly. "Poker?"

"You're on."

They rose at the same time, bumped, brushed. He took her arm automatically, then held on. He tensed, as she did. It wasn't possible to do otherwise. It was possible, barely, to prevent himself from lifting his other hand to her face. She'd done nothing to enhance it today. There was no trace of cosmetics. Her mouth, full, pouty, exciting, was naked. With an effort, he brought his eyes from it, and to hers.

"You're very beautiful, Sunbeam."

It hurt to breathe. She was terrified to move. "I told you not to call me that."

"Sometimes it fits. I've always thought beauty was just an accident of genes or something accomplished through skill. You make me wonder."

"You're a very strange man, Hornblower."

He smiled a little. "You don't know the half of it." He stepped back. "We'd better play cards."

"Good idea." She let out a quiet, relieved breath as she took the deck from a drawer. If she had a little time, alone, she might just figure out what it was about him that jolted her system. "Poker by firelight." She dropped onto the floor. "Now that's romance."

He sat opposite her. "Is it?"

"Prepare to lose."

But he won, consistently, continually, until she began to watch him through narrowed eyes. For lack of anything else, they were playing for cookies, and his pile of chocolate chips kept growing.

"You eat all those you're going to get fat."

He merely smiled. "No, I won't. I have an excellent metabolism."

"Yeah, I just bet you do." With a body like that, he'd have to. "Two pair, queens and fours."

"Mmm." He set his cards down. "Full house, tens over fives."

"Sonofa—" She broke off, scowling, as he raked in the chips. "Look, I don't want to sound like a sore loser, but you've won ten out of twelve hands."

"Must be my lucky night." He picked up the cards and riffled them.

"Or something."

He merely lifted a brow at her tone. "Poker is as much a science as physics."

She snatched up a cookie. "Just deal, Hornblower."

"Are you going to eat your ante?"

Miffed, she tossed it into the pot. "If I don't eat several times a day I get cranky."

"Is that what's wrong with you?"

"I'm basically a very nice person."

"No, you're not." He grinned as he dealt the cards. "But I like you anyway."

"I am nice," she insisted, keeping her face carefully bland when she spotted two aces in her hand. "Ask anybody—except my last two supervisors. Open for two."

Jacob obliged her by adding his two cookies to the pot. He liked her this way—warily friendly, competitive, relaxed, but ready to pounce on any infraction. He supposed it didn't hurt that the firelight painted interesting shadows that played over those fabulous cheekbones. He checked himself—and his hand. This seemed as good a time as any to find out more about her.

"What did you do, before you came here to decide to be a lawyer?"

She made a face, then drew three cards. "I sold underwear. Ladies' lingerie, to be specific." She glanced up, waiting for the disdain, and was mollified when she didn't see it. "I have a drawerful of great stuff I got on discount."

"Oh, really?" He thought about that for a moment, wondering just what her idea of great stuff consisted of.

"Yeah." She was delighted to see that she'd drawn another ace, but she kept her voice even. "The problem was, this particular supervisor wanted you to take the money, box the silks and keep your mouth shut—even when the customer was making an obvious mistake."

He tried to imagine her keeping her mouth shut. He couldn't. "Such as?"

"Such as the pleasantly plump lady who was going to torture herself in a size eight merry widow. Bet three."

"And raise it two. What happened?"

"Well, you open your mouth to make a gentle suggestion and before you know it you've got a pink slip."

"You'd look nice in pink."

She giggled and raised him two more. "No…a pink slip, the boot, the ax. Canned." When he still looked puzzled, she elaborated. "Your services are no longer required."

"Oh. Terminated."

"Right." His term seemed to describe the injustice of it perfectly. "Who needs it?"

"You don't."

She smiled at him. "Thanks. Three aces, pal. Read 'em and weep."

"Straight flush," he countered, and had her sputtering while he piled up more cookies. "You don't have the temperament to work for someone else."

"So I've been told," she muttered. "Several times." She was down to her last five cookies. Her luck, Sunny thought, had been on the down side too long. "But if it's a matter of learning how to adjust or learning how not to eat I'm going to have to go with the first. I don't like being poor."

"I imagine you could do whatever you wanted to do, if you really wanted to do it."

"Maybe." And that had always been the problem. She had no idea what she wanted. She dealt the hand and, deciding to be reckless, went for an inside straight. And ended up with trash. A bluff was always better than a fold, she thought, pushing her miserly pile of cookies into the pot.

He cleaned her out with a pair of deuces.

"Here." Because winning always put him in a good mood, he offered her a cookie. "Have one on me."

"Thanks a lot." She bit into it. "Your luck seems to be on tonight."

"Apparently." He was feeling a bit reckless himself. She looked a great deal more appetizing than the cookies. "We could play one more hand."

"For what?"

"If I win, you make love with me."

Surprised, but determined to keep her poker face intact, she swallowed the bite of cookie. "And if I win?"

"I make love with you."

Popping the rest of the cookie into her mouth, she studied him as she chewed. It would almost be worth it, she mused, to see his face if she took him up on it. Almost worth it, she reminded herself. Either way, she would win. And she would lose.

"I think I'll pass," she said lightly. Rising, she walked over to the sofa, spread herself out on it and went to sleep.

Chapter 6

A blast of music ripped Sunny out of a dead sleep and had her rearing up. When lights blinded her, she groaned and tossed a hand over her eyes in self-defense.

"Who ordered the party?" she asked as Tina Turner roared out rock at top volume.

Jacob, who had dozed off in front of the fire, simply pulled the blanket over his head. Whenever he slept, he preferred to do it like the dead.

Swearing, she pushed herself up off the couch. She had stumbled halfway to the stereo before it dawned on her. "Power!" she shouted, then immediately raced over to sit on Jacob. She heard a muffled grunt from under the blanket and bounced gleefully up and down. "We've got power, J.T. Lights, music, hot food!" When he only grunted again, she poked him. "Wake up, you slug. Don't you know you can be shot for sleeping on sentry duty?"

"I wasn't sleeping. I was bored into catatonia."

"Well, snap out of it, pal. We're back on the circuit." She yanked the cover off his face and grinned when he scowled at her. "You need a shave," she observed. Then, in her delight, she gave him a loud, smacking kiss between the eyes. "How about a hamburger?"

He got a bleary look at her face, all smiles and mussed hair. To his disgust, he felt his body responding. "It can't be more than six in the morning."

"So what? I'm starving."

"Make mine rare." He pulled the blanket over his face again.

"Uh-uh. You have to help." Ruthlessly she ripped the blanket off him again. "Up and at 'em, soldier."

This time he opened only one eye. "Up and at what?"

"It's an expression, Hornblower." She shook her head. "Just how long were you in that lab?"

"Not long enough." Or entirely too long, if all it took to arouse him was a skinny woman sitting on his chest. "I can't get up when you're sitting on me. Besides, I think you broke my ribs."

"Nonsense. I'm ten pounds underweight."

"You wouldn't think so from here."

Too cheerful to be annoyed, she scrambled up, took a firm grip on his forearm and, after some pulling and tugging, dragged him to his feet. "You can make the french fries."

"I can?"

"Sure." To demonstrate her confidence in him, she kept her hand in his and pulled him into the kitchen. "Everything's in the freezer. God, it's cold in here." She rubbed the bottom of one stockinged foot on the top of the other. "Here." She tossed him a bag of frozen fries over her shoulder. "You just dump some on a cookie sheet and stick them in the oven."

"Right." He thought he could figure out the workings of the oven, but he hadn't a clue as to what a cookie sheet might look like.

"Pans are…down there." She gestured vaguely in the direction of a cabinet while she contemplated the package of hamburger.

"The meat's frozen," he pointed out.

"Yeah. Well, we'll have sloppy joes."

"Which are?"

"Delicious," she assured him. Whistling along with the music, she began to rattle pots. Cooking was far down on her list of favorite pastimes, but when push came to shove she was willing to give it her best shot. "Here, use this." She handed him a long, thin piece of metal blackened by heat.

The cookie sheet, Jacob surmised. He went to work. "I don't suppose there's a possibility of coffee."

"Sure. I keep a stash." Still whistling, she dumped the chunk of frozen meat in a pot and set it on low. In moments she had water on to boil and cups waiting. "Heat, hot water, real food." She did a quick little tap dance before digging into a bag of potato chips. "You don't appreciate the little things until you can't have them," she said with her mouth full. "I don't know how people managed before electricity. Imagine having to heat water over an open fire. It must have taken forever."

Jacob was watching the electric ring slowly turn red under the kettle. "Amazing," he agreed, and contemplated just eating the coffee grounds dry.

"Those fries won't cook unless you put them in the oven."

"Yeah." He wished she wouldn't watch him as he studied the dials. The Bake setting seemed safe enough—unless they were supposed to be broiled. He would have given a year of his life for the nutritional center in his lab.

"Spend much time in the kitchen?" Sunny asked from behind him.

"No."

"Who would have guessed?" With a cluck of her tongue, she turned the oven on, then popped the tray inside. "Takes about ten, maybe fifteen."

"Seconds?"

"I love an optimist. Minutes." Because she understood what it was like to wake up ready to chew glass, she patted his cheek. "Why don't you go have a shower? You'll feel better. Most of this should come together by the time you're finished."

"Thanks." As he made his way upstairs he figured it was the nicest thing she'd done for him so far.

He spent a great deal of time cursing the ridiculously archaic workings of her shower. But she was right. He did feel better when he'd accomplished it. Using his ultrasound, he rid himself of his beard. Then he took his daily dose of fluoratyne for his teeth and, curious, poked inside the mirrored cabinet over the sink.

It was a scientific treasure trove. Lotions, potions, creams, powders. A glance at the safety razor made him shudder. The toothbrush made him grin. He saw little puffs of white that appeared to be cotton, thin brushes, tiny pots filled with vividly colored powder.

There was a cream with an exotic name. When he opened the top and sniffed, it was as if Sunny had joined him in the small, steamy room. He made quick work of putting it back on the shelf.

There were pills. A cursory glance showed him that she had them for headaches, body aches, head colds, chest colds. He would make a note to take back a few samples. There was a small plastic case that held a circle of tiny pills that weren't marked at all. Since they were half gone, he assumed they were something she took regularly. That concerned him. He didn't like to think that she was ill. Replacing them, he wondered how he might ask her about her medication.

He started downstairs, then simply followed the scents. He didn't know what she could have done with the hunk of frozen meat, but it smelled like heaven. And there was coffee. No perfume could have been sweeter. She handed him a cup as he walked in the door.

"Thanks."

"It's okay. I know how it feels."

He sipped, giving her a clinical study over the rim. Her eyes were clear, and her color was good. She looked perfectly healthy. In fact, he couldn't remember ever having seen anyone healthier. Or more alluring.

"When you look at me like that I feel like a germ under a microscope."

"Sorry. I was just going to ask how you felt."

"A little stiff, a lot hungry, but basically okay." She tilted her head. "How about you?"

"Fine. I had a headache," he said, suddenly inspired. "I took some of your pills."

"Okay."

"The ones in the little blue case weren't marked."

Her eyes widened, rolled, then filled with laughter. "I don't think they'd do you much good."

"But you need them?"

This time she closed her eyes and shook her head.

"And he calls himself a scientist. Yeah, you could say I need them. Better safe than sorry, right?"

Baffled, but losing ground, he nodded. "Right."

"Then let's eat."

She had plates by the range with buns open on them. Using a generous hand, she scooped the saucy meat into them, tossed a heap of fries beside it and was done. She didn't speak again until she'd worked her way through half the meal.

He watched her dump a stream of white crystal from a pottery tube on her potatoes. He shook some on his own experimentally. Salt, he discovered. The real thing. Though the taste was wonderful, he resisted the temptation to use more and wondered about her blood pressure. If he could have figured a way, he would have popped her into the medilab on the ship for a checkup.

"I guess we're going to live."

He wasn't sure what he was eating, but she was right again. It was delicious. "It stopped snowing."

"Yeah, I noticed. Listen, I hate to say it, but I'm glad you were here. I'd have hated to be here alone the last couple of days."

"You're pretty self-sufficient."

"But it's better when you have somebody to fight with. I never asked…do you plan to hang around until Cal and Libby get back? It could be weeks."

"I came to see him. I'll wait."

She nodded, wishing his answer hadn't relieved her. She was getting entirely too used to his company. "I guess you must be in a position to take as much time off as you like."

"You could say that time is exactly what I do have. How long are you staying?"

"I'm not sure. It's too late to get into school this semester. I thought I might write to some colleges. Maybe I'll try the East Coast. It would be a change." She sent him a quick, hesitant smile. "How would I like Philadelphia?"

"I think you would." He wondered how to describe it to her so that she would understand. "It's beautiful. The historic district is very well preserved."

"The Liberty Bell, Ben Franklin, all that."

"Yes. Some things last, no matter what else changes." Though it had never mattered much to him before. "The parks are very green and shady. In the summer they're full of children and students. The traffic's miserable, but that's all part of it. From the top of some of the buildings you can see the entire city, the movement, the old and the new."

"You miss it."

"Yes. More than I'd imagined." But he was looking at her, seeing only her. "I'd like to show it to you."

"I'd like that, too. Maybe we can talk Cal and Libby into flying out. You could have a real family reunion."

She saw his expression change and instinctively laid a hand over his. "Did I say something wrong?"

"No."

"You're angry with him," Sunny murmured.

"It's personal."

But she wasn't going to be put off. He wasn't the snarling idiot she had first assumed him to be. He was just confused. If there was one trait she shared equally with her sister, it was the inability to turn away a stray.

"J.T., you must see how unfair it is to resent Cal for falling in love and getting married, for starting a life here."

"It's not that simple."

"Of course it is." This time, she promised herself, she would not lose her temper. "They're both adults, and they're certainly able to make up their own minds. Besides, well, they're wonderful together." He sent her a silent, cynical look that infuriated her. "They are. I've seen them with each other. You haven't."

"No." He nodded. "I haven't."

"That's nobody's fault but—" She caught herself, ground her teeth and went on, more calmly. "What I'm trying to say is that I might not have known Cal before he became part of the family, but I know when someone's happy. And he is. As for Libby—he does something for her no one else ever has. She's always been so shy, so easily pushed into the background. But with

Cal she just glows. Maybe it's not the easiest thing to accept that someone else is the best thing that ever happened to a person you love—but you have to accept it when it's true."

"I don't have anything against your sister." Or, if he did, he intended to keep it to himself for the time being. "But I intend to talk to Cal about the change he's made in his life."

"You really are bullheaded."

He considered the description and decided it was apt enough. "Yes." He smiled at her, delighted by the sulky mouth, the lifted chin. "I'd say we both are."

"At least I don't go around poking my nose into other people's affairs."

"Not even pleasantly plump women who want to torture themselves into…what was it—a Merry Widow?"

"That was entirely different." With a sniff, she pushed her plate away. "I may be cynical, but even I believe in love."

"I never said I didn't."

"Oh, really?" Her lips curved, because she was sure she had backed him into a corner. "Then you won't interfere if you see that Cal and Libby are in love."

"If they are, I hardly could, could I? And if they're not—" he gestured, palm up "—then we'll see."

She steepled her fingers, measured him. "I could

always send you back into the forest, let you freeze in your sleeping bag."

"But you won't." He toasted her with his coffee cup. "Because, underneath the prickly hide, you're basically kindhearted."

"I could change."

"No, you couldn't. People don't, as a rule." Abruptly intense, he leaned forward to take her hand. It was a gesture he didn't make often, and one that he couldn't resist at that moment. "Sunny, I don't want to hurt your sister. Or you."

"But you will. If we're in your way."

"Yes." He turned her hand over thoughtfully. It was narrow, and surprisingly soft and delicate for one that packed such a punch. "You have strong family feelings. So do I. My parents…they've tried to understand Cal's decision, but it's difficult for them. Very difficult."

"But they've only to see him for themselves to understand."

"I can't explain." He shifted his eyes from their joined hands to hers. "I wish I could. More than I can tell you."

"Are you in trouble?" she blurted out.

"What?"

"Are you in trouble?" she repeated, tightening her fingers on his. "With the law, or something."

Interested, he kept his hand in hers. Her eyes were

huge and drenched with concern. For him. He couldn't remember ever being more touched. "Why would you think so?"

"The way you've come here… I guess the way you haven't come before. And you act… I don't know how to explain. You just seem so out of place."

"Maybe I am." It should have been amusing, but he didn't smile. If he hadn't been so sure he would regret it, he would have pulled her into his arms and just held on. "I'm not in trouble, Sunny. Not the way you mean."

"And you haven't been—" she searched for the most delicate way to approach the subject "—ill?"

"Ill?" Baffled, he studied her. The light dawned, slowly. "You think I've been—" Now he did smile, and surprised them both by bringing her hand to his lips. "No, I haven't been ill, physically or otherwise. I've just been busy." When she tried to draw her hand away, he held on. "Are you afraid of me?"

Pride had always been her strongest suit. "Why should I be?"

"Good question. You wondered if I was—" he gestured again "—unbalanced. But you let me stay. You even fed me."

The uncharacteristic gentleness in his voice made her uncomfortable. "I'd probably have done the same for a sick dog. It's no big deal."

"I think it is." When she pushed away from the table, he rose with her. "Sunbeam."

"I told you not to—"

"There are times when it's irresistible. Thank you."

She was more than uncomfortable now. She was unnerved. "It's okay. Forget it."

"I don't think so." Gently his thumb stroked over her knuckles. "Tell me, if I had said I was in trouble, would you have helped?"

She tossed her head carelessly. "I don't know. It would depend."

"I think you would." He took both her hands and held them until she was still. "Simple kindness, especially to someone away from home, is very precious and very rare. I won't forget."

She didn't want to feel close to him. To be drawn to him. But when he looked at her like this, with such quiet tenderness, she went weak. There was nothing more frightening than weakness.

"Fine." Fighting panic, she shook her hands free. "Then you can return the favor and do the dishes. I'm going for a walk."

"I'll go with you."

"I don't—"

"You said you weren't afraid of me."

"I'm not." She let out a long-suffering breath. "All right, then, come on."

The moment she opened the door, the cold stole her breath. The wind had died down and the sun was fighting through the layers of high clouds, but the air was like brittle ice.

It would clear her head, Sunny told herself. For a moment in the kitchen, with him looking so intently into her eyes, she'd felt as though… She didn't know what she'd felt. She didn't want to.

It was enough to be free to walk, though the snow was up to her knees. Another hour of confinement and she'd have gone mad. Perhaps that was what had happened to her in there, with him. A moment of madness.

"It's wild, isn't it?"

She stood in what had been the backyard and looked out on acres of solid white. The dying wind moaned through the trees and sent powdery snow drifting.

"I've always liked it best in the winter. Because if you're going to be alone you might as well be completely alone. I forgot the bird food. Hang on."

She turned, wading through the snow. He thought she moved more like a dancer now than an athlete. Graceful despite the encumbrances. It worried him to realize that he'd been content to watch her for hours. In a moment she was trudging back, dragging an enormous burlap sack.

"What are you doing?"

"Going to feed the birds." She was out of breath but

still moving. "This time of year they need all the help they can get."

He shook his head. "Let me do it."

"I'm very strong."

"Yes, I know. Let me do it anyway."

He took the sack, braced, put his back into it and began to haul it across the snow. It gathered snow—and weight—with every step.

"I thought you weren't a nature lover."

"That doesn't mean I'd let them starve." And she'd promised Libby.

He hauled the bag another foot. "Couldn't you just dump it out?"

"If a thing's worth doing—"

"It's worth doing well. Yeah, I've heard that one."

She stopped by a tree and, standing on a stump, began to fill a big wood-and-glass house with seed from the sack. "There we go." She brushed seed from her hands. "Want me to carry it back?"

"I'll do it. Why any self-respecting bird would want to hang around here in the middle of nowhere I can't understand."

"We're here," she called out as he hauled the sack across the snow.

"I can't understand that, either."

She grinned at his back, and then, not being one to waste an opportunity, she began to ball snow. She had a good-size pile of ammunition when he came out again, and she sent the first one sailing smack into his forehead.

"Bull's-eye."

He wiped snow out of his eyes. "You've already lost at one game."

"That was poker." She picked up another ball, weighed it. "This is war. And war takes skill, not luck."

He dodged the next throw, swearing when he nearly overbalanced, then caught the next one in the chest. Dead center.

"I should tell you I was the top pitcher on my softball team in college. I still hold the record for strike-outs."

The next one smacked into his shoulder, but he was prepared. In a move she had to admire, he came up with a stinging fastball that zoomed in right on the letters. He'd pitched a few himself, but he didn't think he would mention that he'd been captain of the intergalactic softball team three years running.

"Not bad, Hornblower." She sent out two, catching him with the second on the dodge. She had a mean curve, and she was pleased to note that she hadn't lost her touch. Snow splattered all over his coat. One particularly well-thrown ball nearly took off his hat.

Before her pile began to dwindle, she had him at eight

hits to two and was getting cocky. It didn't occur to her that he had closed half the distance between them.

When he took one full in the face, she doubled over with laughter. Then she shrieked when he caught her under the arms and lifted her off her feet.

"Good aim, bad strategy," he commented before he dropped her face first in the snow.

She rolled over, spitting out snow. "I still won."

"Not from where I'm standing."

With a good-natured shrug, she held out a hand. He hesitated. She smiled. The moment he clasped her hand, she threw her weight back and had him flying into the drift beside her.

"What does it look like now?"

"Hand-to-hand."

He grasped her by the shoulders. They only sank deeper. Snow worked its way, cold and wet, down the collar of his borrowed coat. He found it, and the way her body twisted and turned against his, impossibly stimulating. She was laughing, kicking up snow as she tried to pin him on the icy mat. Breathless, she managed a half nelson, and she nearly had the call when she felt herself flying over his shoulder.

She landed with a thump, half buried, and lay there for a second, dragging in air. "Nice move," she panted. Then she dived at him again. She scissored, dipped and managed to slither out of his hold. Working fast, she twisted until she was half sitting, half lying on his back. Using her weight, she dunked his face in the snow.

"Say uncle."

He said something a great deal ruder, and she laughed so hard she nearly lost her grip.

"Come on, J.T., a real man admits it when he's licked."

He could have beaten her, he thought in disgust as his face numbed. But twice when he'd tried for a hold his hand had skimmed over particularly interesting curves. It had broken his concentration.

"Two out of three," he mumbled.

"If we try for two out of three, we'll freeze to death." Taking his grunt for agreement, she helped him turn over. "Not bad for a scientist."

"If we took it indoors, you wouldn't have a chance." But he was winded.

"The point is, I came out on top."

He lifted a brow. "In a manner of speaking."

She only grinned. "I wish you could see your face. Even your eyelashes are white."

"So are yours." He lifted a gloved hand that was already coated with snow and rubbed it on her face.

"Cheat."

"Whatever works." Exhausted, he let his hand drop again. He didn't know the last time he'd been taken— or when he'd enjoyed it so much.

"We'd better get some more wood." She braced a hand to get up, slipped and landed with a thump on his chest. "Sorry."

"It's all right. I've got a few ribs left."

His arms had come around her. His face was close. It was a mistake, she knew, to stay this way, even for a moment. But she didn't move. And then she didn't think. It was the most natural thing in the world for her to lower her lips to his.

They were cool, and firm, and everything she wanted. Kissing him was like diving headfirst into a cold mountain lake. Thrilling, exhilarating. And risky. She heard her own sound of pleasure, quick and quiet, before she threw what was left of caution to the winds and deepened the kiss.

She winded him. Weakened him. Loss of control meant nothing. Control was meant to be given up in passion. But this...this was different. As her lips heated his, he felt both will and strength drain away. There was a mist in his brain as thick and as white as the snow they lay in. And he could think of nothing and no one but her.

The women who had come before her were nothing. Shadows. Phantoms. When her mouth slid agilely over his he understood that there would be no women after her. She had, in one heady instant, taken over his life. Surrounded it, invaded it. Consumed it.

Shaken, he brought his hands to her shoulders, prepared, determined, to hurl her aside. But his fingers only tightened, and his need only grew.

It was like a rage in him. She could feel it. It was building in her, as well. A fury. A driving hunger. And his mouth, his mouth alone, was dragging her over the rocky border between heaven and hell. So close, she thought, that she could feel the flames licking at her skin, tempting her to tumble recklessly into the fire. For it would be all brimstone and heat with him. And she was afraid, very afraid, that she would never be satisfied with less.

She lifted her head, an inch, then two. She was amazed to find her mind spinning and her breath uneven. It had only been a kiss, she reminded herself. A kiss, however passionate, didn't alter lives. Still, she wanted distance, and quickly, so that she could convince herself she was the same person she had been before it.

"We really have to get that wood," she managed. Suddenly she was terrified that she wouldn't be able to stand. It wouldn't do her ego a bit of good to have to crawl back to the house. Cautiously she rolled away from him. Then, using every ounce of will she possessed, she dragged herself to her feet. She made a production out of brushing the snow from her coat and wished he would say something. Anything.

"Look."

Wary, she turned. But he was only pointing to the feeder, where a few hardy birds were enjoying breakfast. It helped her relax a little. "Well, I've done my duty by them." Because she was suddenly and brutally aware of the cold, she gave herself a quick shake. "I'm going in."

She waded across the snow. They didn't speak again as they gathered wood, as they tromped snow from their boots or as they carried the logs to the woodbox. Sunny banked down an urge for a steaming cup of tea. She wanted to be alone. She wanted to think.

"I'm going up for a shower." Feeling miserably awkward, she watched him toss logs on the fire.

"Fine."

She made a face at his back. "Fine."

He waited until he heard her climb the stairs before he straightened. The woman was scrambling his brain, he decided. It was highly probable that he was still disoriented from the trip. That was why she was having such a profound effect on him. All he needed was a little more time to adjust. Data or no data, it would be best if he took that time aboard ship.

He took a long, thoughtful look at the cabin. Still, he'd promised to do the dishes. It would be an interesting experience to try his hand at it.

Upstairs, Sunny stripped off layers of clothes, letting each item fall carelessly to the floor. Naked, she turned the shower on, letting it run until the hot water was steaming. She winced as she stepped under it, then let out a long, lazy sigh.

Better, she told herself. It was certainly a better way of getting her blood moving than kissing Jacob. No, it wasn't.

She laid her forehead against the wall of the shower and with her eyes closed let the water rain over her.

Maybe she'd been a little crazy when she'd kissed him, but she'd never felt more alive. She couldn't blame him, not this time. She had made the move. She had looked into his eyes and known he was the one.

Yet how could he be? She barely knew him, was far from convinced she trusted him. Half the time she was sure she disliked him. But… But, she thought again. The other half of the time she was afraid she was falling in love with him.

It was completely irrational, undeniably foolish and totally genuine. All she had to do was figure out what to do about it.

Pouring shampoo into her palm, she tried to think. She was a practical woman. As far back as her memory took her, she had been able to take care of herself. Problems, even emotional ones, were meant to be surmounted. If she was falling in love, she would deal with it. The trick was not to do anything rash.

Caution, common sense and control, Sunny decided. She lathered her skin lavishly. She would keep a practical distance from Jacob until she got to know him better, until she was more certain of her feelings. It made perfect sense. More confident now, she turned under the spray and let the water sluice the suds from her.

Once she had determined her own feelings, she would work on his. There was no denying he was a strange sort of man. Interesting, certainly, but different in ways she had yet to fully figure out.

She could handle him. After turning off the water, she slicked a hand down her hair. She had always been able to handle men very satisfactorily. In this case, she just had to handle herself first.

Satisfied, she kicked her clothes out of the way. Dry, she wrapped a towel around her and stepped out into the hall.

He'd enjoyed doing the dishes. It was just the sort of mindless chore he'd needed to relax his mind. And his body. The plastic squeeze bottle marked dishwashing liquid claimed to contain real lemon juice. He took a sniff of his hands and found the lingering scent pleasant. As soon as he got back to the ship he was going to make a report on it.

And the task had given him time to put his reaction to Sunny in perspective. Being attracted to her was natural, even elemental. But he was intelligent enough to control certain primal urges. Particularly when acting on them would cause incredible complications.

She was beautiful, desirable, but she was also impossible. The idea of pursuit had been a bad one. He was well aware now that a physical encounter with her would not be simple. It could only be problematic. He would solve the problem for both of them by gathering up his things and spending the bulk of his time on his ship. When Cal came back he would convince his brother that he had made a mistake. Then they would go home, where they belonged. And that would be the end of it.

It should have been. Perhaps it would have been. But he came to the top of the stairs just as Sunny stepped out of the bath. She held a towel at her breasts with both hands. He gripped the rail so hard that he wondered how the wood didn't crumble under his fingers.

Bad timing. The thought went through both of their heads. Or perhaps it was perfect timing.

Chapter 7

He crossed to her slowly, soundlessly. Inevitably. In his eyes she saw mirrored her own needs. A reflection of desires, raw and ready, that she had refused to acknowledge. Even now, faced with them, she wanted to deny that they existed. Not with this power. Not with this potency.

She could have held up a hand, said one simple word. *No.*

Perhaps it would have stopped him. Perhaps not. But her hands remained clutched on the towel. And she said nothing. At all.

At her back she could feel the steam from the shower still rising. Or was it anticipation that heated her skin? Her fingers were balled tight, lodged in the subtle valley between her breasts. Her eyes were steady on his.

But her pulse scrambled erratically, as if she had just crossed the finish line of a long, arduous race.

He didn't touch her. Not at first. He already knew that once he did, the time to turn back would be lost for both of them. A part of him wished desperately that he could simply walk back, turn away and continue on the route he already had mapped out. She was a detour, a dangerous combination of curves that would only lead him astray.

But, looking at her, his eyes dark and intent on her face, he knew that his bridges were already smoking behind him.

He touched her face...took it in his hands. Cupped it, molding his fingers to the angles, as if to mold the shape of it in his mind. To remember her, always, as she was in this one instant, to remember her through all the centuries that would keep them apart.

He heard her breath catch, then release, felt the faint, almost delicate, tremblings of passion still restrained. All the while he watched her, measuring that look in her eyes. Part panic, part challenge. Resisting her would be as impossible as stopping his own heartbeat at will.

Slowly, deliberately, he spread his fingers, skimming them up so that his palms slid over her jawline, her cheekbones, her temples, until his hands were caught in her wet, sleek hair. He took one fistful of it, then two.

Her gaze never faltered from his. She wouldn't permit it to. But she couldn't prevent a quick, soft gasp as he drew her head back. Her lips parted, in both invitation and acceptance, as he leaned closer. Only the thinning mist from the bath wound between them.

With his mouth a breath away from hers, he stopped, waited. It had nothing to do with hesitation. There was as much challenge in his eyes as in hers.

To meet it, she moved forward, the slight sway of her body closing the narrow distance between them.

"Yes," she said, and lifted her mouth to his.

No single word could have lit the fires so quickly. No practiced seduction could have broken the last chains on his control. His fingers tightened in her hair, and his mouth swooped down on hers.

The glory of it. He felt hunger answer hunger, desperation ply desperation. Her mouth was like an oasis, offering the last cool drop of life to a dying man who knew he must stumble back into the sun. She appeased even as she incited, promised even as she demanded. There was honey for the taking, rich and thick, but always at the risk of being stung. The risk made the reward all the sweeter.

He had never known a woman could make him suffer, and make him relish the pain, all from a meeting of lips.

Her hands were trapped between their bodies. They

flexed, impatient, not for release but to take as he was taking. She spread them flat on his chest, fretting for freedom. But her murmur of protest was lost in his assault on her mouth before it merged with a groan of pleasure.

His teeth nipped and nibbled, and then his tongue plunged deep, greedily. Deaf and blind to all else, she dived in, as recklessly as he.

Her hands were free for an instant. Before she could clutch at him, her world seemed to tilt, and she was swept up in his arms. Swept off her feet, she thought giddily. No man before him had ever dared to attempt it. No man before him would have succeeded. With muscles like iron, he caught her hard against him, closing the distance to the bedroom in a few long-legged strides. Even as she tugged at his sweater, they were tumbling onto the bed.

With one frantic stroke, he ripped the towel from her, then gripped her seeking hands in his, fingers interlacing, locking, so that he could look his fill. The thin winter light seeped through the window to lie loverlike on her skin.

Her struggle to free her hands stopped. For a moment, she thought her breathing had, as well.

He knew his had. It wasn't air that rushed through him, but a desire so acute it left him reeling.

She was pale as moonlight, long limbed, with the

fine-toned muscles of a dancer or an athlete. The strength was there, and the femininity. As he looked, and looked, and looked, she began to tremble.

Her hair was dark, wet and slicked back from her face. Now, as they had earlier with anger, her eyes had deepened to smoke. And they watched him.

With her hands still caught in his, he lowered his mouth. She arched, as greedy as he for the contact. Even as the kiss pumped through her like a drug, she tried to tug her hands free. But he was relentless, as if he knew that once he released her the power would be taken from him. Not to dominate, but only to pleasure, he kept her prisoner.

She moaned as the soft cotton of his sweater brushed her skin. She wanted his flesh against hers. She wanted her hands on him, and his on her. But he used his mouth, only his mouth, to drive her to the edge of reason.

Rapidly, almost savagely, he moved his lips over her—her face, her neck, her shoulders. She spoke his name, writhing frantically beneath him, but he moved restlessly on.

With openmouthed kisses he circled her breasts, tormenting himself as much as her. Then he drew the point into his mouth to nip, to suck, to stroke with the rough edge of his tongue.

He had known the flavor of women, but hers was new, so exclusively hers that he knew that if he supped of ten times ten thousand others, he would never be satisfied. Never had he known so keen or so perfect a match. The ache to claim all of her sprinted inside him.

"Jacob." His name was like a prayer that was transformed into a frantic moan. "Let me—"

But the words ended on a stunned, suffocated cry as he shot her over a towering, airless peak. She flew, thoughts and feelings tangling and breaking apart. Still his hands were locked with hers. Gasping, giddy, she closed her eyes as her tensed muscles went lax.

If this was pleasure, she had never tasted it before. If this was passion, she understood for the first time why a woman would die for it.

Dazed, she opened her eyes. The fierce triumph in his had her heart pounding against her ribs again. "I can't—I haven't—"

"You can, and you will. Again." And he watched, ravenous, as he sent her soaring.

Shudders racked her. Each movement of her body beneath his pushed her closer to the edge of reason. Freed, her hands slid bonelessly to the rumpled sheets. There was a mist in front of her eyes. As his hands joined his mouth in plundering her, she wondered that she didn't simply float up and away into it.

Touch me.

She wasn't certain if he spoke the words or if his need merely echoed in her head. Through layers of drugged pleasure she lifted her arms, brought him close. And found his mouth with hers.

Strength raced back into her, edgier, more potent, from the weakness. A new level of desperation had her dragging his sweater over his head. Twin gasps of pleasure speared the quiet as her hands found him.

Warm, firm. Hers. She stroked and explored as thoroughly, as mercilessly, as he. Catapulted by a hunger grown insatiable, she rolled with him on the bed, her mouth fused to his, tearing at his jeans with frantic fingers until heated flesh met heated flesh.

He had thought he knew what delights a woman could bring when she touched a man. But *she* had never touched him before. All he had known, all he had experienced before, paled. And meant nothing.

He was filled with her body, mind and soul. She was everything he'd dreamed of without knowing he was dreaming, everything he'd wished for without knowing he was wishing. As her lips ran over him, small, hungry sounds rising in her throat, desire built to a rage.

Over and over they rolled on the bed, legs tangling as they pushed each other from brink to brink. The war they fought was punctuated by searing kisses, bruising strokes. Driven beyond reason, he gripped her hips. But she was already rising to meet him, to take him in.

Sheathed inside her, he felt the first shudders, hers, his, rip through them. Her legs locked around him. His fingers dug into the sheets. Reason shattered. Rhythms matched.

And he was rocketing through space, through time. All he knew was that she was with him.

She lay crossways on the bed, one arm flung out, the other hand still clutched in Jacob's hair. His body was as limp as hers as he sprawled over her, his head resting between her breasts. His first thought was that her heart, thudding under his ear, matched the pace of his own. Before reason could set in, he slid a hand over the warm tangle of sheets and covered hers. He knew he would never be able to describe the sensation that rippled through him as her fingers curled against his.

He was heavy. She didn't care. It seemed perfectly feasible that she could spend the rest of her life lying just so, listening to his breathing and to the quiet sound of snow melting from the eaves in the sun.

So this was what it was to love, she mused. She hadn't known she'd waited all her life to feel like this. It had always seemed possible to her to live her life alone, independent, content with the freedom to do as she pleased when she pleased.

The idea of sharing a bed with a man you cared for, respected, understood, had seemed practical and certainly human enough. But the idea of sharing a life— or needing to share it because you couldn't imagine living without one person—had always struck her as romantic nonsense.

No more.

And he was such a beautiful man. Strong and smart. Stubborn and opinionated. Exactly, she realized, the kind of man she needed. Without any one of those qualities, her personality would have driven her to run right over him, making both of them miserable. Because he had them, she would run into him often, bruising them both. And she'd be wildly happy.

Smiling, she caught herself stroking his hair. After letting out a careful breath, she made herself stop. What did a woman like her do with these tender feelings? She understood passion. At least she understood it now. But what about this soft, yielding sensation, this dependence, this need to nurture and cherish and simply love? How would a man like Jacob Hornblower react to this sudden gush of emotion?

He'd sneer at her. Closing her eyes, she admitted that she would have sneered herself only hours before.

But everything had changed. For her, Sunny reminded herself. If she was honest she would accept the fact that she'd started falling the moment she'd faced him, ready to fight, in this very same room.

But Jacob… She herself had called him a tough nut. Cracking him, discovering whether there was indeed a soft center capable of gentler emotions, would be a difficult task. It would take effort, she thought. That was no problem. It would take patience. That was.

Oblivious of where her thoughts were headed, he turned his head enough to brush a kiss to the curve of her breast.

"Your taste," he murmured.

"Hmm?"

"It keeps me hungry." He scraped his teeth along her skin, then smiled when he felt her heart skip a beat. "I like you here best." He propped himself up to study her face lazily. "Naked and in bed."

"A typical male attitude." Deliberately she danced her fingers down his hip and watched his eyes darken. "But then, I think I prefer you in the same state."

"It's convenient that we finally agree about something." He shifted so that he could trace her lips with the tip of his tongue. "I like your mouth, Sunbeam. It's stubborn and sexy."

"I could say the same about yours."

"We agree again."

"A new record." She caught his lower lip between her teeth. "We could push our luck. What else do you like?"

"Your…" His smile spread slowly. "…energy."

"Another winner."

With a laugh, he deepened the kiss. She was just as sweet, and just as potent, as the first time. "Your body," he decided. "I definitely like your body."

She sighed into his mouth. "We're on a roll, J.T. Don't stop now."

He shifted his attention to her earlobe. "This is a nice spot," he murmured, nuzzling until they were both dizzy. "But I suppose, under the circumstances, I can confess that I find your mind…intriguing."

"Intriguing," she repeated, as shudder after delicious shudder passed through her. "An interesting choice of words."

"It seemed more apt than infuriating at the moment. And I…" His words trailed off when he spotted a line of faint bruises on her shoulder. He placed the tips of his fingers on them experimentally. "I've marked your skin," he said, surprised and a bit appalled. If he had bruised her during a fight, he wouldn't have given it a second thought. But in bed, while loving…that was a different matter. "I'm sorry."

She twisted her head to glance at them. She certainly hadn't felt them. "Are you?"

He looked back to see her lips curved in what he considered a typically female smile. "No, I suppose I'm not."

"Under the circumstances," she supplied.

"Right." He started to speak again, to make some joke, but found himself suddenly and totally at a loss for words. Something in her smile, in her half-hooded eyes, in the tilt of that damn-you chin, turned his brain to mush.

Ridiculous, he told himself as he continued to stare at her. Absolutely and completely ridiculous. Whatever he was feeling, it couldn't be love—not the kind of love that caused men to make foolish and life-altering decisions. It was affection, he told himself. Attraction, desire and passion, tempered with a certain amount of caring, perhaps. But love. He had no room for it. And no time.

Time. Reality struck him like a blow. Time was the biggest obstacle of all.

He started to push himself away, to put some distance between them until he could think clearly again. Still smiling, she wrapped arms and legs around him. "Going somewhere?"

"I must be heavy."

"You are." She continued to smile, then traced her lips with her tongue. Her hips moved gently, sinuously, against his. Thrilled, she watched his eyes cloud as he grew inside her. "I was hoping we could do a little experiment."

He shook his head but failed to clear it. "Experiment?"

"Physics." She trailed a single fingertip down his back. "You know about physics, don't you, J.T.?"

He used to. "That's Dr. Hornblower to you," he muttered, and buried his face in her throat.

"Well, Doc…isn't there this theory about an object in motion remaining in motion?"

His breath was ragged in her ear. "Let me show you."

She ached all over. And she'd never felt better in her life. Bleary-eyed, she winced at the intruding sunlight. Morning. Again, she realized.

She wouldn't have believed it was possible to spend the better part of a day and all of a night in bed. With only snatches of sleep. With a grumbling sigh, she tried to roll over and met the solid wall of Jacob's body.

He'd been busy since dawn, she mused. Busy working her over to the edge of the bed. Now he took up ninety percent of the mattress, along with all of the sheets and blankets. The only thing saving her from sliding onto the floor was the weight of the leg he had hooked around her hips. And the arm stretched carelessly, and certainly not amorously, over her throat.

She shifted again, met the unmoving line of resistance and narrowed her eyes. "Okay, pal," she said under her breath, "we're going to begin as I mean to go on, and I don't mean to roll onto the floor every night for the rest of my life."

She gave him an unloverlike nudge in the stomach

with her elbow. He swore and shoved her another inch toward the edge.

Tactics, Sunny decided. She changed hers by sliding a hand intimately over his hip and thigh. "J.T.," she whispered, trailing a line of kisses down his cheek. "Honey."

"Hmm?"

She nibbled delicately at his ear. "Jacob? Sweetheart?"

He made another vague sound and cupped her breast. Sunny's brow lifted. His movement had cost her another precious fraction of an inch.

"Baby," she added, figuring she was running out of endearments. "Wake up, sugar. There's something I want to do." Gently, seductively, she brushed her lips down to his shoulder. "Something I really need."

As his lips curved, she bit him. Hard.

"Ow." His eyes flew open, temper and bafflement warring in them. "What the hell was that for?"

"So I could get back my share of the bed." Satisfied, she snuggled into the pillow he'd just vacated. She opened one eye and was gratified to see that he was scowling at her. "Anyone ever tell you you're a bed hog? And a blanket thief." She snatched the loose cover and rolled into it.

"You're the first one to complain."

She only smiled. She was counting on being the last.

Frowning, he rubbed the wound on his shoulder. There were shadows under her eyes. They made her look vulnerable. The faint throbbing where her teeth had connected reminded him that she was anything but.

Inside that angular body was a whirlwind of energy. All wells of passion that he was sure—even with the marathon they'd put each other through—had yet to be tapped. She'd taken him places he hadn't believed existed. Places he was already yearning to return to. In the deepest part of the night she had been insatiable, and impossibly generous. He'd had only to touch her to have her respond. She'd had only to touch him to cause the need to churn.

Now, in the full light of morning, she was wrapped in the blankets, with only her tousled cap of hair and half of her face in view. And he wanted her.

What was he going to do about her? With her? For her? He hadn't a clue.

He wondered how she would react if he told her everything. She'd go back to thinking he was unbalanced. He could prove it to her. And once he had they would both have to face the fact that whatever had happened between them during the last spin of the earth on its axis was transient. He wasn't ready for that.

For once in his life he wanted to delude himself. To pretend. They would have only a few weeks together at best. More than other men, he had firsthand knowledge of how fickle time could be. So now he would use it, and take what he had with her.

But how could he? Sitting up, he rubbed his hands over his face. It wasn't fair to her. It was grossly unfair, particularly if his instincts were correct and her feelings were involved. Not telling her would hurt her when it ended. Telling her would hurt her before it had really begun. And maybe that was best.

"Going somewhere?" she asked him.

He was reminded of when she had used the same phrase before, and where it had ended. Now he thought of how he could tell her just how far away he was going. She was an intelligent woman. He had only to give her the facts.

"Sunny."

"Yes?" She ran a hand up his arm. Then, feeling repentant, she rose long enough to kiss his shoulder where she had bitten it.

"Maybe this shouldn't have happened." He saw by the way her smile faded that he'd begun badly.

"I see."

"No, you don't." Annoyed with himself, he made a grab for her before she could roll out of bed.

"Don't worry about it," she said stiffly. "When you've been fired as often as I have you get used to rejection. If you're sorry about what happened—"

"I'm not." He cut her off with a brisk shake that turned the glazed hurt in her eyes to smoke.

"Don't ever do that again."

"I'm not sorry," he said, struggling for calm. "I damn well should be, but I'm not. I can't be, because all I can think about is making love with you again."

She blew her hair out of her eyes and swore to herself that she would be calm. "I don't know what you're trying to say."

"Neither do I." He released her to tug his fingers through his hair. "It mattered," he blurted out. It wasn't what he'd meant to say, but it, too, was a fact. "Being with you mattered to me. I didn't think it would."

The ice she had deliberately formed around her heart melted a little. "Are you upset because it was more than sex?"

"I'm upset because it was a hell of a lot more than sex." And he was a coward, he realized, because he couldn't tell her that what they had now would end before either of them was ready. "I don't know how to handle it."

She was silent for a moment. He looked so angry—with himself. And as confused as she was by what had grown—no, by what had exploded into life—between them. "How about one day at a time?"

He shifted his gaze to hers. He wanted to believe it

could be that simple. Needed to. "And what happens when I leave?"

The ice had definitely melted, because she felt the first slash in her heart. "Then we'll deal with it." She chose her words carefully. "Jacob, I don't think either of us wanted to get involved. But it happened. I wouldn't want to take it back."

"Be sure."

She lifted a hand to his cheek. "I am." Afraid she would say too much too soon, she bundled back under the covers. "Now that that's settled, it's your turn to make breakfast. You can yell up the stairs when it's ready."

He said nothing. The thought of what might tumble from his heart to his lips unnerved him. If it was a choice between saying too much and saying too little, he had to choose the latter. He rose, tugged on what clothes came to hand, and left her.

Alone, she turned her face into the pillow. It smelled of him. Letting out a long, weary sigh, she willed her body to relax. She had lied. Rejections wounded her deeply, left her miserable and aching and full of self-loathing. A rejection from him would hurt so much more than the loss of a job.

Rubbing her cheek on the pillowcase, she watched the slant of sunlight. What would she do if he ended it? She would recover. She needed to believe that. But she knew that if he turned away from her, recovery would take a lifetime.

So she couldn't let him turn away.

It was important not to push. Sunny was very aware that she demanded too much from the people close to her. Too much love, too much attention, too much patience, too much faith. This time it would be different. She would be patient. She would have faith.

It would be easier, she knew, because he was as unsteady as she. Who wouldn't be, with the velocity and force with which they had come together? If they could progress so far in such a short time, how much further could they go in the weeks ahead?

All they needed was a little time, to get to know each other better, to work on those rough edges. Forget the rough edges, she thought, gazing at the ceiling. Those would take a couple of lifetimes, at least. In any case, she rather liked them.

But time…she was certain she had that right. Time was what they needed to get used to what had happened, to accept that it was going to keep right on happening.

She smiled at that, her confidence building again. And if that didn't work she'd browbeat him into it. She knew exactly what she wanted. And that was a first. She wanted Jacob T. Hornblower. If, after he had seen and spoken with Cal, he packed his pitiful little bag and headed back east, she would just go after him.

What was a few thousand miles between friends? Or lovers.

Oh, no, he wasn't going to shake her off without a fight. And fighting was what she did best. If she wanted him—and she was certain she did—then he didn't have a chance. She had as much right to call things off as he did, and she was far from ready. Maybe, if he was lucky, she'd let him off the hook in fifty or sixty years. In the meantime, he was just going to have to deal with it, and with her.

"Sunny! This stuff is in the bowls, and I can't find the damn coffee."

She grinned. Ah, the sweet sound of her lover's voice carrying on the morning air. Like music, like the trilling of birds—

"I said, I can't find the damn coffee."

Like the roar of a wounded mule.

Madly in love, she tossed the heap of blankets aside.

"It's in the cupboard over the stove, dummy. I'll be right down."

Chapter 8

Another week of quiet, serenity and nature in the rough would drive Sunny mad. She'd already accepted that. Even love wasn't enough of a buffer against hour after hour of solitude, punctuated only by the occasional call of a hardy bird and the monotonous drip, drip, drip of snow melting from the roof.

For variety she could always listen to the wind blow through the trees. When she had stooped that low she realized that she would gladly trade all of her worldly possessions for the good grinding noise of rush-hour traffic in any major city.

A girl might be born in the woods, she thought, but that didn't mean you could keep her there.

Jacob was certainly a distraction, an exciting one. But as the days passed it became clear that being snow-bound in a log cabin in the middle of nowhere was no more his definition of a good time than it was hers. The fact that she found that a relief didn't ease the boredom.

They managed to occupy their time. Arguing, in bed and out. Two restless personalities stuck in the same space were bound to strike sparks. But their minds were as restless as their bodies and needed stimulation.

Sunny compensated by hibernating. Her reasoning was, she couldn't be bored if she was asleep. So she developed the habit of taking long naps at odd hours. When he was certain she was asleep, Jacob would slip out, taking advantage of the bonus he'd found in the shed. Cal's aircycle. With that he would make a quick trip to his ship and input new data into the main computer.

He told himself that he wasn't deceiving her, he was simply performing part of the task he had come to her time to accomplish. And if it was deceit, it couldn't be helped. He'd nearly convinced himself that what she didn't know couldn't hurt her. At least for the time being.

Though he was as restless as she, he found himself storing up memories, images, moments. The way she looked when she woke—sleepy-eyed and irritable as a child. The way she'd laughed, the sun shining on her hair, when they'd built a house of snow under the pine trees. The way she felt, passion humming under her skin, when they made love in front of the fire.

He would need them. Those memories, those remembrances of each conversation or spat. Each time he returned to the ship he was reminded of just how much he would need them. He told himself he was only preparing to go on with his life. And so was she.

She had written inquiries to the handful of universities she'd selected. But the weather had so far prevented her from venturing out as far as Medford to mail them. She had read, lost to Jacob at poker, even dragged out her sketchbook in desperation. When she tired of drawing the view of snow and pine trees from the windows, she sketched the interior of the cabin. Bored, she resorted to drawing caricatures.

Jacob read incessantly, and he'd taken to scribbling in a spiral notebook he'd dug out of some drawer. When Sunny asked him if he was preparing for an experiment, he made noncommittal noises. When she pressed him, he simply pulled her into his lap and made her forget to ask questions.

They lost power twice, and they made love as frequently as they argued. Which was often.

Sunny was certain, when she caught herself making the bed for lack of anything better to occupy her time, that if they didn't *do* something they would both find themselves in a home for the gently deranged.

Leaving the bed half-made, she sprinted to the top of the stairs. "J.T."

He was currently trying to keep himself sane by building a city of cards. "What?"

"Let's drive to Portland."

Jacob's attention was fixed on a particularly intricate arrangement. He thought the structure was beginning to resemble the skyline on Omega II.

"J.T."

"Yeah." With fingers that were rock-steady, he added another card.

"I guess it's too late," Sunny murmured, and sat down to the west of the city. "He's already gone around the bend."

"Do we have any more of these?"

She sighed at his dwindling stack of cards. "Nope."

"I was thinking of a bridge."

"Think shock therapy."

"Or maybe a skybelt."

"A what?"

He caught himself and put another card in place. "Nothing. My mind was wandering."

She snickered. "What's left of it."

"You were saying?"

"I was saying let's get out of Dodge."

"I thought Medford was the closest town."

She opened her mouth, closed it again. "Sometimes,"

she said at last, "I'm not sure if you belong on the same planet with the rest of us."

"It's the right planet." A portion of his pasteboard roof fluttered. "Breathe the other way, will you?"

"Jacob. If you could spare a moment of your valuable time."

He glanced up then, and he had to smile. "You have the sexiest pout I've ever seen."

"I don't pout." When she caught herself doing just that, she hissed between her teeth and blew down a building.

"You've just murdered thousands of innocent people."

"There's only one person I'm going to murder." Desperate, she grabbed a handful of his sweater. "J.T., if I don't get out of here I'm going to start bouncing off the walls."

"Can you do that?"

"Just watch me." She leaned closer. "Portland. People, traffic, restaurants."

"When do you want to leave?"

With a huff, she sat back again. "You *were* listening."

"Of course I was listening. I always listen. When do you want to leave?"

"A week ago. Now. I can be ready in ten minutes."

She sprang up. Though Jacob winced when his city collapsed, he rose with her. "What about the snow?"

"It hasn't snowed for three days. Besides, we have four-wheel drive. If we can get to Route 5, we're home free."

The thought of getting out nearly made him forget his priorities. "And if Cal comes back?"

She was all but dancing with impatience. "They're not due back for a couple of weeks. Anyway, they live here." Carelessly she stepped on his demolished city. "J.T., think carefully. Do you really want to see a grown woman turn into a raving lunatic?"

"Maybe." Taking her by the hips, he pulled her intimately close. "I like it when you rave."

"Then prepare to enjoy yourself."

"I am." He dragged her to the floor.

She argued—briefly. "I'm going," she said, undoing the buttons of her flannel shirt.

"Okay."

"I mean it."

"Right." He tugged the plain white undershirt over her head.

She struggled but couldn't prevent her lips from curving. Giving up, she helped him off with his sweater. "And so are you."

"As soon as you're finished raving," he promised, then closed his mouth over hers.

Sunny threw a small bag into the back of the Land Rover. She'd taken time to grab a toothbrush, a hairbrush, her favorite camisole and a lipstick. "In case we have to stop on the way," she explained.

"Why would we?"

"I don't know how long it's going to take us to get out of the mountains." She settled in the driver's seat. "It's about five hours after that."

Five hours. It took them five hours to get from one part of a single state to another. For the past few days he'd nearly forgotten how different things were.

She shot him a look, eyes bright, lips curved. "Ready?"

"Sure."

It was difficult not to stare as she turned a small key and sent the combustion engine roaring. He could feel the vibration through the floorboards. A few small adjustments, he mused, and even an archaic vehicle could be made to run smoothly and quietly.

Jacob was on the brink of pointing this out to her when she shoved the Land Rover in gear and sent snow spitting out from under the tires.

"All right!"

"Is it?"

"This baby rides like a tank," she said happily as they lumbered away from the cabin.

"Apparently." He braced himself, finding it incongruous that he should worry about life and limb here, when he had taken countless trips at warp speed. "I suppose you know what you're doing."

"Of course I know what I'm doing. I learned how

to drive in a Jeep." They labored up an incline where snow had melted and refrozen into a slick surface. Jacob judged the height and breadth of the trees. He could only trust that she knew how to avoid them.

"You look a little green." She had to chuckle as they plowed, then fishtailed, then plowed again, making erratic but definite progress. "Haven't you ever ridden in one of these?"

He had an image of driving his own LSA vehicle— Land, Sea or Air. It was smooth and quiet and as fast as a comet. "No, actually, I haven't."

"Then you're in for a treat."

The Land Rover bumped over rocks hidden under the snow. "I bet."

They forged through the drifts. He nearly relaxed. By all indications, she knew how to handle the vehicle. Such as it was. After the first twenty minutes, the heater began to hum.

"How about some tunes?"

His brow creased. "Fine," he said cautiously.

"You're in charge."

"Of what?"

"Of the tunes." She navigated carefully down an incline. "The radio."

He eyed a particularly large tree. At their current rate and angle, he estimated thirty seconds to impact. "We didn't bring it."

"The car radio, J.T." She missed the tree by six or eight inches. "Pick a station."

She'd taken her hand from the wheel for an instant to gesture at the dashboard. Eyes narrowed, Jacob studied it. Trusting luck, he turned a dial.

"It works better if you turn it on before you try to tune in a station."

Biting back an oath, he tried another dial and was greeted by a blast of ear-popping static. After adjusting the volume, he applied himself to the tuner. His first stop was an instrumental melody, loaded with strings, that made him cringe. Still, he glanced over at Sunny.

"If that's your choice, we'll have to reassess our relationship immediately."

Sound faded in and out as he played with the tuner. He hit on some gritty rock, not too dissimiliar from what might have sounded over the airwaves in his own time.

"Good choice." She turned her head briefly to smile at him. "Who's your favorite musician?"

"Mozart," he answered, because it was partially true and undeniably safe.

"You're going to like my mother. When I was a kid, she used to weave to his *Clarinet Concerto in A Minor.*" With the radio still rocking, she hummed a few bars. "For the purity of sound, she'd always say. Mom's always been big on pure—no additives, no preservatives."

"How did you keep food fresh without preservatives?"

"That's what I say. What's life without a little MSG? Anyway, then Dad would switch on Bob Dylan." She laughed, more relieved than she wanted to admit when they turned onto the first plowed road. "One of my earliest memories of him is watching him weed his garden, with his hair down to his shoulders and this scratchy Dylan record playing on a little portable turntable. 'Come gather 'round, people, wherever you roam.' All he was wearing—Dad, not Dylan—was bell-bottoms and love beads."

Jacob got an uncomfortable flash of his own father, dressed in his tidy gardening clothes, blue shirt, blue slacks, his hair carefully trimmed under a stiff peaked cap, his face quiet as he hand-pruned his roses and listened to Brahms on his personal entertainment unit.

And of his mother, sitting in the shade of a tree on a lazy Sunday afternoon, reading a novel while he and Cal had tossed a baseball and argued over strike zones.

"I think you'll like him."

Dragged back, Jacob blinked at her. "What?"

"My father," she repeated. "I think you'll like him."

He battled down the anger that had risen up inside him. It was simple enough to put two and two together. "Your parents live in Portland?"

"That's right. About twenty minutes from my place." She let out a quiet, satisfied breath as they turned onto

Route 5 and headed north. "They'll be glad to meet you, especially since Cal's family has been so shrouded in mystery."

The friendly smile she offered him faded when she saw his expression. When her hands clenched on the wheel it had nothing to do with anger and everything to do with despair.

"Meeting my parents is not synonymous with a life-time commitment."

Her voice was stiff and cold. If he hadn't been so lost in his own unhappiness, he would have heard the hurt beneath it.

"You didn't mention visiting your parents." The fact was, he didn't want to meet them, or to think of them as people.

"I didn't think it was necessary." Her clutch foot began to tap on the floorboards. "I realize your idea of family differs from mine, but I wouldn't think of coming back to town and not seeing them."

Bitterness rose like bile in his throat. "You have no idea what family means to me."

"No?" She gave a quick, moody shrug. "Let's just say I can surmise that you don't have a problem cutting certain members of it out of your life for extended periods. Your business," she said before he could re-tort. "And you're certainly not obligated to come with me when I go to see my family." Her fingers began to tap in time with her foot. "In fact, I'll be happy not to even mention your name."

He was careful not to speak again. If he did, too much of what he was feeling would pour out, leaving too much to be explained.

She didn't know how he felt. It was all so easy, so straightforward, for her. All she had to do was hop into this excuse for transportation and spend a few hours on what passed for a roadway. And she could see her family. By using the current system of communication she could speak with them over relatively long distances. Even if she decided to travel to the other side of the planet, some element of twentieth-century technology would provide a link.

She knew nothing of separation, of losing a part of yourself and not knowing why. How would she react if she found herself faced with the possibility of never seeing her sister again?

She wouldn't be so damn smug then.

For the next hour or so, Jacob amused himself by sneering at the other vehicles on the road. Ridiculously clumsy, slow and absurdly inefficient. Carbon monoxide pumping into the atmosphere. Gleefully poisoning their own air. They had no respect, he thought. For themselves, their resources, their descendants.

And she thought he was insensitive.

He wondered what would happen if he strolled into

what passed for a research lab in this age and showed them the procedure for fusion.

They'd probably sacrifice a lamb and make him a god.

He sat back, arms crossed. They'd just have to figure it out for themselves. Right now, his biggest problem was keeping warm, with all the cold air blowing off of Sunny.

He frowned when she pulled out onto a ramp. He hadn't been paying close attention, but he was certain they hadn't driven for five hours. "What are you doing?"

"I'm going to get something to eat and put gas in the car." She snapped the words off without a glance at him.

Hugging her resentment to her, she pulled into a gas station, got out and slammed the door behind her. As she reset the self-service pump, she muttered under her breath.

She'd forgotten how his mind worked. Obviously he was deluding himself into believing that she was luring him into some sort of trap. *I want you to meet my parents. How do you feel about a double-ring ceremony?* Sunny ground her teeth. It was insulting.

Maybe she was in love with him—and that was a situation she dearly hoped could be reversed—but she hadn't done one single thing to pressure him. Or to lead him to believe that her heart was all aflutter at waiting for him to get down on one knee.

If he thought she'd intended to flaunt him in front of her parents like so much matrimonial beefcake, he had another think coming. The jerk.

Jacob sat a moment, then decided to get out to stretch his legs. And get a look at his surroundings.

So this was a refueling station, he mused, studying the gas pumps. Sunny had stuck the nozzle end of a hose into a compartment on the side of the Land Rover. From her expression, she didn't look too happy about standing out in the cold with her hand on the switch. Behind her, the pump—the gasoline pump, he elaborated—clicked as numbers turned over. The odor of fuel was strong.

Other cars crowded the pump islands. Some waited in their vehicles for a man in a cap to come out and go through the procedure Sunny was doing for herself. Others did as she was, and shivered in the cold.

He watched a woman bundle a trio of children around the side of a building that was set farther off the road. The children were arguing and whining, and the woman was snatching at arms. He had to grin. At least that much hadn't changed over time.

On the road, cars chugged by. Jacob wrinkled his nose at the stench of exhaust. A sixteen-wheeler roared by, leaving a stream of displaced air in its wake.

There were plenty of buildings, such as they were. Tall ones, squat ones, all huddled together as if they were afraid to leave too much room between them. He found the style uninspired. Then, less than a block down the street, he spotted something that brought him a pang of homesickness. A pair of high golden arches. At least they weren't completely uncivilized, he thought. He was grinning when he turned back to Sunny.

She didn't respond.

Ignoring him, she screwed the gas cap in place and hung up the hose. Silent treatment or not, he told himself, he would not apologize for something that was so clearly her fault. Still, he followed her into the building and was distracted by rows of candy bars, shelves of soft drinks and the prevalent scent of crude oil.

When she took out paper money, Jacob had to stick his hands in his pockets to keep himself from reaching out to touch it. The man in the cap ran grimy fingers over the keys of a machine. Red numbers appeared in a viewbox. The paper was exchanged, and Sunny was given metal disks.

That was money, too, Jacob reminded himself. Coins, they were called. He was frustrated when she dumped them in her bag before he could get a close look. He wondered how he could approach her for some samples.

The woman he'd seen earlier herded the three children inside, and the room was immediately filled with noise. All three fell greedily on the rows of candy bars.

"Just one," the woman said, an edge to her voice. "I mean it." She was digging in her purse as she spoke.

The children, bundled in coats and hats, set up an arguing din that ended in a shoving match. The smallest went down on her bottom with a thump and a wail. Jacob bent automatically to set her on her feet, then handed her the smashed candy bar. Her bottom lip was quivering, and her eyes, big and round and blue, were filled to overflowing.

"He's always pushing me," she complained.

"You'll be as big as they are pretty soon," he told her. "Then they won't be able to push you around."

"Sorry." Sighing, the woman picked her daughter up. "It's been a long trip. Scotty, you're going to sit on your hands for the next ten miles."

When Jacob turned to leave, the little girl was smiling at him. And so, he noted, was Sunny.

"Are you talking to me again?" he asked as they walked back to the car.

"No." She tugged on her gloves as she sat in the driver's seat. It would have been easier to go on hating him if he hadn't been so sweet with the little girl. "I'm a great deal harder to charm than a three-year-old."

"We could try a neutral subject."

She turned on the engine. "We don't have any neutral subjects."

She had him there. He lapsed into silence again as she merged with traffic. But he could have kissed her when she turned into those golden arches.

She followed a sign that said *Drive-thru* and stopped at a board that listed the restaurant's delicacies. "What do you want?"

He started to ask for a McGalaxy Burger and a large order of laser rings, but he didn't see either on the menu. Once again he put his fate in her hands. "Two of whatever you're having." Because he couldn't resist, he toyed with the hair at the back of her neck.

Annoyed, she shook his fingers off. She spoke into the intercom, listened for the total, then joined the line of cars waiting to be served. "We'll make better time if we eat while we drive."

They inched forward. "Are we in a hurry?"

"I don't like to waste time."

Neither did he, and he wasn't sure how much more they had together. "Sunny?"

No response.

"I love you."

Her foot slipped off the clutch. Her other slammed the brake pedal when the Land Rover stalled. The car was still rocking as she turned to gape at him. "What?"

"I said I love you." It didn't hurt as much as he'd

thought it would. In fact, it felt good. Very good. "I figured we might as well have it out in the open."

"Oh." As responses went, it wasn't her best. But she was staring straight ahead into the rear window of the car in front. There was a stuffed cat suction-cupped to the glass. It was grinning at her. The car behind her gave an impatient beep of the horn and had her fumbling with the ignition key. Rattled, she pulled up to the service window.

"Is that all you can say?" Annoyance colored his tone as she turned to blink at him. "Just 'Oh'?"

"I…I'm not sure what…"

"That'll be 12.75," the boy shouted through the window as he held out white paper bags.

"What?"

He rolled his eyes. "It's 12.75. Come on, lady."

"Sorry." She took the bags, dumped them in Jacob's lap. Even as he swore at her, she dug out a twenty and passed it to the boy. Without waiting for her change, she pulled into the first available parking space and stopped the car.

"I think you singed my—"

"Sorry," she snapped, cutting him off. Because she felt like a fool, she rounded on him. "It's your own fault, Mr. Romance, dropping something like that on me while I'm stuck in a line of cars at a fast-food drive-in. What did you expect me to do, throw myself in your arms while they were adding on the pickles?"

"I never know what the hell to expect from you." He reached into the bag, brought out a foil-wrapped burger and tossed it to her.

"From me?" She unwrapped the burger and took a huge bite. It did nothing to ease the fluttering of her stomach. "From me? You're the one who started this, Hornblower. One minute you're snapping my head off, the next you're telling me you love me, and then you're throwing me a cheeseburger."

"Just shut up and eat." He shoved a paper cup into her hand.

He'd bite off his tongue before he'd say it to her again. He didn't know what had come over him. Gasoline fumes, undoubtedly. No man in his right mind could fall in love with such an obstinate woman. And— no help from her—he was still in his right mind.

"A few minutes ago you were begging me to talk to you," she pointed out, sucking on her straw.

"I never beg."

She turned then, eyes smoky. "You would if I wanted you to."

He could have strangled her then, for saying what he realized was no more than the truth. "I thought we were going to drive while we ate."

"I changed my mind," she said tightly. The way her

insides were shaking, she wasn't sure she could navigate ten feet. She'd be damned if she'd let him know it. Since it wasn't possible to kick him, due to their position, she simply turned and stared through the windshield.

She continued eating mechanically and cursed him for spoiling her appetite.

Imagine, telling her that he loved her while they were waiting for hamburgers. What style, what finesse. She tapped her fingers on the wheel and bit back a sigh. How incredibly sweet.

Cautious, she cast a sidelong look at him. His profile was set, his eyes were steely. She had seen him angrier, she supposed, but it was a close call. Something about the way he fumed in frustrated silence made her feel incredibly sentimental. Twenty years from now she would look back and smile over the way he had said those magic words the very first time.

She scrambled onto her knees and threw her arms around him. He gasped as cold liquid splashed on his knees. "Damn it, Sunny, you've spilled it all over me."

He squirmed, then stilled when her mouth found his. He tasted her laughter on the tip of her tongue. Hampered by the gearshift, he struggled to drag her closer.

"Did you mean it?" she demanded, shoving what was left of their lunch aside.

No way was he going to let her off that easily. "Mean what?"

"What you said."

He settled her awkwardly in his lap, making sure her bottom came in direct contact with his wet knees. "Which time?"

Her breath came out in a huff, but she curled her arms around his neck. "You said you loved me. Did you mean it?"

"I might have." He worked his hands up under her coat but had to be content with the flannel of her shirt. "Or I might have been trying to start a conversation."

She bit his lip. "Last chance, Hornblower. Did you mean it?"

"Yes." God help them both. "Want to fight about it again?"

"No." She rested her cheek against his. "No, I don't want to fight. Not right now." He felt her sigh move through her body. "It scared me."

"That makes two of us."

After pressing a kiss to his throat, she drew back. "It gets even scarier. I love you, too."

He'd known it, and yet— And yet, hearing her say it, seeing her eyes as she spoke, watching her lips form the words, nothing could have prepared him for the force of feeling that poured into him. A waterfall of emotion. Tumbling through it, he pulled her mouth to his.

He couldn't bring her close enough. It didn't seem odd that they were huddled inside a car in a parking lot beside a busy street in broad daylight. Much odder was the fact that he was here at all, that he had found her, despite the centuries.

When he lived, she couldn't go. When she lived, he couldn't stay. And yet, in this small space of time, they were together.

Time was passing.

"I don't know what we're going to do about this," he murmured. There had to be a way, some equation, some theory. But what computer could analyze data that was so purely emotional?

"One day at a time, remember?" She drew back, smiling. "We've got plenty of time." She hugged him close, and she didn't see the trouble come into his eyes. "Speaking of which, we've got almost two hours before Portland."

"Too long."

She chuckled, then squirmed back into her seat. "I was thinking the same thing."

She zoomed out of the lot, keeping her eyes peeled. With a grin of satisfaction, she pulled into the first motel she spotted. "I think we can use a break." After snatching up her bag, she strolled into the office to register.

This time she used a plastic card—something much

less foreign to him. With little trouble and less conversation, she secured a key from the clerk.

"How long have we got?" Jacob asked as he swung an arm over her shoulder.

She shot him a look. "It may be a motel," she said, steering them toward a door marked 9, "but I don't think this particular chain rents rooms by the hour. So…" She turned the key in the lock. "We've got the rest of the day—and all night—if we want."

"We want." He caught her the moment she stepped inside. Then, wheeling her around, he used their joined bodies to slam the door closed. Because his hands were already occupied, Sunny reached behind her to secure the chain.

"J.T., wait."

"Why?"

"I'd really prefer it if we drew the drapes first."

He ran the palm of one hand over the wall, searching for a button while he tugged at her coat with the other.

"What are you doing?"

"Looking for the switch."

She chuckled into his throat. "At thirty-five a night you have to close the curtains by hand." She wiggled away to deal with it. "I'd love to see the kind of motels you're used to."

The light became dim and soft, with a thin, bright slit in the center, where the drapes met. She was standing just there, with the light like a spear behind her. And she enchanted him.

"There's this place on an island off Maine." He shrugged out of the borrowed coat, then sat down to pry off his boots. "The rooms are built on a promontory so that they hang over the sea. Waves crash up beneath, beside, in front. The windows are…" How to explain it? "They're made out of a special material so that you can see out as far as the horizon but no one can see in—so that beyond one entire wall there's nothing but rock and ocean. The tubs are huge and sunken, and the water steams with perfume."

He rose slowly, picturing it. Picturing her there, with him. "You can have music, just by wishing for it. If you want moonlight, or the sound of rain, you've only to touch a switch. The beds are big and soft, so that when a man reaches for his woman she all but floats to him over it. While you're there, time stops for as long as you believe it."

Aroused, she let out a shaky breath. "You're making this up."

He shook his head. "I'd take you there, if I could."

"I have a good imagination," she said as he pushed the coat from her shoulders. She shuddered when he ran his hands down her. "We'll pretend we're there. But I don't think there's moonlight."

Smiling, he eased her down and pulled off her boots one by one. "What then?"

"Thunder." Her breath shivered out when he trailed his fingers up her calf. "And lightning. That's what I feel when you touch me."

There was a storm in him. He saw the power of it reflected in her eyes. She rose so that her body skimmed up his, inch by tormenting inch. Before he could take her lips, she was pressing them, already hot, to his throat. The pulse that hammered there excited her, the taste inflamed her. Wanting more freedom, she pushed his sweater up and up, then let it fall to the floor in a heap.

With a lingering sound of pleasure, she traced her lips over his chest, absorbing the texture, the intimate flavor, of his skin. It was soft, dreamily soft, over the hard ridges of muscles. His scent, earthy and male, delighted her.

There was thunder. She could feel it when she let her mouth loiter over his heart. It beat for her. There was lightning. She saw the flash of power when she looked into his eyes.

He was surprised he could still stand. What she was doing was making him dizzy and desperate. Those long, lovely fingers already knew his body well. But every time they explored they found new secrets.

And her mouth... He gripped her shoulders as she

took her lips on a lazy journey down his chest, over the quivering muscles of his stomach. Her tongue left a moist trail. Her throaty laugh echoed in his head.

He felt her fingers on the snap of his jeans, and the denim as it slid from waist to hipbone. Pleasure arrowed into him, its point jagged.

Time didn't stand still. It reeled backward until he was as primitive as the men who had forged weapons from stone. With an oath, he dragged her up into his arms, his mouth branding hers, all fire and force.

Then she was under him on the bed, her body as taut as wire. Her breath heaved, seemed to tear out of her lungs, as his hands raced over her. Possessed. She could hear him speak, but the roaring in her head masked the words. Driven, he ripped her shirt down the front, sending buttons flying. Wild to touch her, he hooked his fingers in the collar of the thin cotton beneath it and tore it aside.

She called out his name, stunned, elated, terrified by the violence she had brought out in him. Then she could only gasp, fighting for air, for sanity, as the first climax rocketed through her. But there was no weakness this time.

Energized, she reared up, enfolding him so that they were half sprawled, half kneeling, on the bed. Torso to torso, hip to hip. With her head thrown back, she let him take his mouth over her, pleasuring, receiving pleasure.

Like a madman, he tore, pulled, dragged at her jeans, until her body was as naked as his. Her hands slid off his slick skin as she tried to draw him to her. It was then that she realized that he was shuddering, his body vibrating with a need even she hadn't guessed at.

She started to speak his name, but he was inside her, filling her, firing her. His muscles were taut as he braced her against him, letting her frenzy drive them both.

Faster, deeper, as she soared over wave after wave. Passion became abandonment as her body bowed back, tempting his eager mouth to feast on her. Sensation layered over sensation until they were all one torrid maze of light and color and sound. As he pulled her back, his body thrust inside hers, she no longer knew where she began and he stopped. She forgot to care.

Chapter 9

Sunny unlocked the door to her apartment, ignoring the faint creak behind her that meant Mrs. Morgenstern had cracked her own door to watch the comings and goings on the third floor.

She had chosen the third floor, despite the vagaries of the elevator and the nosiness of the neighbors, because the tiny apartment boasted what passed for a balcony. On it there was just room enough for a chair, if she angled it so that she sat with her ankles resting on the rail. It overlooked the parking lot.

It was good enough for her.

"This is it," she announced, a bit surprised by the surge of nostalgia that filled her at the sight of her own things.

Jacob stepped in behind her. Sunlight poured through

the skinny terrace doors to his right. Pictures marched along the walls—photographs, sketches, oil paintings and posters. Even in her own rooms, Sunny preferred company.

Piles of vibrantly colored pillows were heaped on a sagging, sun-faded sofa. In front of it was a table piled with magazines, books and mail—opened and unopened. In the corner, a waist-high urn held dusty peacock feathers.

Across the room was another table that Jacob recognized as a product of expert workmanship from an even earlier century. There was a fine film of dust on it, along with a pair of ballet shoes, a scattering of blue ribbons and a broken teapot. A collection of record albums were stuffed into a wooden crate, and on a high wicker stool stood a shiny china parrot.

"Interesting."

"Well, it's home. Most of the time." She shoved the paper bag she was carrying into his arms. It contained the fresh supply of cookies and soft drinks they'd picked up along the way. "Put these in the kitchen, will you? I want to check my machine."

"Right. Where?"

"Through there." She gestured, then disappeared through another door.

He had another moment's pause in the kitchen. It

wasn't just the appliances this time. He was growing used to them. It was the teapots.

They were everywhere, covering every available surface, lining a trio of shelves on the walls, sitting cheek by jowl on top of the refrigerator. Every color, every shape, from the tacky to the elegant, was represented.

It had never occurred to him that she was a collector, of anything. She'd always seemed too restless and unrooted to take the time to clutter her life with things. Strangely, he found it endearing to realize that she had pockets of sentimentality.

Curious, he studied one of her teapots, a particularly florid example of late twentieth-century— He couldn't bring himself to call it art. It was squat, fashioned out of inferior china, with a bird of some kind on the lid and huge, ugly daisies painted all over the bowl. As a collector's item, he decided, it had a long way to go.

He set it aside and went to explore.

The blue ribbons were prizes, he discovered. For swimming, fencing, riding. It seemed Sunny had spent a lifetime scattering her talents. Her name was signed— scrawled, really—on some of the pictures on the walls. Sketches of cities, paintings of crowded beaches. He imagined many of the photographs were hers, as well.

There was more talent there, showing a clear eye and a sharp wit. If she ever settled on any one thing, she was bound to shoot right to the top. Oddly enough, he preferred her just as she was, scattering those talents, experimenting, digging for new knowledge. He didn't want her to change.

But she had changed him. It wasn't easy to accept it, but being with her, caring for her, had altered some of his basic beliefs. He could be content with one person. Compromises didn't always mean surrender. Love didn't mean losing part of yourself, it meant gaining that much more.

And she had made him wonder how he was going to face the rest of his life without her.

Turning toward the bedroom, he went to find her.

She was standing in what he first took for a closet. Then when he saw the bed, he realized it was the entire room. Though it was no more than eight by eight, she had crammed something into every nook and cranny. More books, a stuffed bear in a virulent orange, ice skates. A set of skis hung on the wall like sabers.

The dresser was crowded with bottles, at least twenty different brands of scent and lotion. There was also a photograph of her family.

He found it difficult to concentrate on it, as she was standing by the bed, stripped to the waist. She had taken off his sweater. He'd been forced to loan it to her for the remainder of the trip, as he'd destroyed her shirt. With one ear cocked toward the unit by her bed that served as radio, alarm clock and message machine, she rooted through her closet for another top.

"Hey, babe." The voice on the machine was cajoling and very male. The moment he heard it, Jacob despised it. "It's Pete. You're not still steamed, are you, doll? Come on, Sunny, forgive and forget, right? Give me a call and we'll go dancing. I miss that pretty face of yours."

Sunny gave a quick snort and dragged out a sweatshirt.

"Who's Pete?"

"Whoa." She put a hand between her breasts. "You scared me."

"Who's Pete?" he repeated.

"Just a guy." She tugged the sweatshirt on. "I was hoping you'd bring in one of those sodas." She sat on the bed to pull off her boots.

"Sunny." This time the voice on the phone was smooth and feminine. "We got a postcard from Libby and Cal. Let us know when you get back in town."

"My mother," Sunny explained, wriggling her toes. Grinning, she passed him the sweater. "You can have this back now."

Not entirely sure what he was feeling, he took off his coat. Beneath it, his chest was bare. As he started to pull the sweater over his head, the machine announced the next message.

"Hey, Sunny, it's Marco. Where the hell are you, sweet thing? I've been calling for a week. Give me a buzz when you get back." There was a sound, like a big, smacking kiss before the beep.

"Who's Marco?" Jacob asked, deadly calm.

"Another guy." Her brows rose when he took her arm and pulled her to her feet.

"How many are there?"

"Messages?"

"Men."

"Sunny…Bob here. I thought you might like to—"

Deliberately Sunny shut off the machine. "I haven't kept track," she said evenly. "Do you want to compare past lives, J.T.?"

He didn't answer, because he found he couldn't. Releasing her, he walked away.

Jealousy. It filled him. And how he detested it. He didn't consider himself a reasonable man, but he was certainly an intelligent one. He knew she hadn't begun to live the moment he had walked into her life. A woman like her, beautiful, bright, fascinating, would attract men. Many men. And if it had been possible he would have murdered each and every one of them for touching what was his.

And not his.

He swore and spun around to see her watching him from the doorway.

"Are we going to fight?"

He ached. Just looking at her, he ached, for what was, and for what could never be. "No."

"Okay."

"I don't want them near you," he blurted out.

"Don't be a jerk."

He reached her in three strides. "I mean it."

She tugged her arms free and glared at him. "So do I. Damn it, do you think any of them could mean anything to me after you?"

"If you don't—" Her words sunk in and stopped him. Lifting his hands, palms out, he stepped back. She stepped forward.

"If I don't what? If you think you can give me orders, pal, you've got another think coming. I don't have to—"

"No, you don't." He cut her off, taking her balled fist in his hand. Not his, he reminded himself. He was going to have to start getting used to that. "I'm not handling this well. I've never been in love before."

The fighting light died from her eyes. "Neither have I. Not like this."

"No, not like this." He brought her fingertips to his lips. "Just review the rest of your communications later, will you?"

Amused by his phrasing, she grinned. "Sure. Listen, help yourself to whatever's in the kitchen. The TV's in the bedroom, the stereo's out here. I'll be back in a couple of hours."

"Where are you going?"

She picked up a pair of discarded sneakers and tugged them on. "I'm going to go see my parents. If you're up to it later, maybe we can have a real dinner out and go dancing or something."

"Sunny." He took her hand as she picked up her coat. "I'd like to go with you."

Solemn eyed, she studied him. "You don't have to, Jacob. Really."

"I know. I'd like to."

She kissed his cheek. "Go get your coat."

William Stone stalked to the door of his elegant Tudor home in bare feet. His sweatshirt bagged on his long, skinny frame. The knees of his jeans had worn through, but he refused to give them up. In one hand he carried a portable phone, in the other a banana.

"Look, Preston, I want the new ad campaign to be subtle. No dancing tea bags, no heavy-metal music, no talking teddy bears." On a sound of frustration he yanked the door open. "Yes, that includes waltzing rabbits, for God's sake. I want—" He spotted his daughter and grinned from ear to ear. "Deal with it, Preston," he ordered, and broke the connection. "Hi, brat." He spread his arms and caught her on a leap.

Sunny gave him a noisy kiss, then stole his banana. "The tycoon speaks."

William grimaced at the portable phone. Such pretensions embarrassed him. "I was just..." His words trailed off when he spotted Jacob on the threshold. He searched his mind for a name. Sunny often brought men to the house—friends and companions. William refused to think of his little girl having lovers. Though this one looked familiar, he couldn't place the name.

"This is J.T.," Sunny said between bites of banana. She had her arm around her father's waist.

Two peas in a pod, Jacob thought, pleased that he'd been able to dig up the expression. The same coloring, the same bone structure, the same frank, measuring looks. Taking the initiative, Jacob stepped forward and offered a hand.

"Mr. Stone."

Since one arm was still holding his daughter—a bit possessively—William stuck the phone in the back pocket of his jeans before he shook Jacob's hand.

"Hornblower," Sunny continued, enjoying herself. "Jacob Hornblower. Cal's brother."

"No kidding." The handshake became more enthusiastic, the smile more friendly. "Well, it's nice to see you. We were beginning to think Cal had made up his family. Come on in. Caro's around somewhere."

He released Jacob but kept a firm hold on Sunny as

he led the way through the foyer into the living room. Jacob got the impression of bold colors mixed with pastels. And, again, elegant. A simple, timeless elegance.

A few pieces of glittery crystal, gleaming antiques and, of course, what he now realized was Caroline Stone's stunning art. If Jacob was surprised to find her woven masterpieces so casually displayed on the walls, he was speechless to see another spread on the floor as a rug.

"Have a seat," William was saying as he walked thoughtlessly over what Jacob considered a priceless work of art. "How about a drink?"

"No, nothing. Thank you." He was staring at an ornamental lemon tree in the window. His own father nurtured the same type of plant.

"You'll have to have tea," Sunny said, patting Jacob's hand as she sat on the sofa beside him. "If you don't, you'll hurt Daddy's feelings."

"Of course." He glanced up at William again and caught his narrowed-eyed, speculative look.

The phone in William's back pocket rang. He ignored it. Recognizing the gleam in her father's eye and wanting to delay the questions for the time being, Sunny dropped the banana peel in his hand. "I'd just love some, Daddy. How about Oriental Ecstasy?"

"Fine. I'll take care of it."

He disappeared through a doorway, the phone still shrilling in his pocket.

Sunny chuckled and put her hand on Jacob's again. "I suppose I should warn you…" She tilted her head, curious. Jacob was gawking—she couldn't think of another word for his expression—at one of her mother's wall hangings. "J.T.? Would you like to tune in?"

"Yes. What?"

"I was going to warn you, my father's nosy. He'll ask you all kinds of questions, most of them personal. He can't help it."

"All right." He couldn't resist. Rising, he walked over to the rectangle of cloth and ran his fingers over the soft material and bleeding colors.

"Beautiful, isn't it?"

"Yes, it's very beautiful."

She got up to stand beside him. "She's become a very well respected artist."

Respected was a mild word for Caroline Stone. Her work was found behind glass in museums. It was studied and revered by art students throughout the settled universe. And he was here, running his fingers over an exquisite piece of it.

"She used to sell blankets and things for grocery money."

"That's a myth."

"I beg your pardon?"

"Nothing." He dropped his hand, shoved it into his pocket. For the first time since he had stepped off the ship he felt totally disoriented. These were people he had learned about from study disks. Historical figures. Yet he was here, in their home. He was in love with their daughter. How could he be in love with a woman who had lived, and died, centuries before he had been born?

Panic. He tasted it. Turning, he gripped her arms. Reality, solid and warm. He was holding it in his hands. "Sunny."

"What's wrong?" He was so pale, and his eyes were so dark. "What is it?"

He just shook his head. There was nothing he could say. No words he knew to explain it. Instead, he brought his mouth down on hers and let her flavor chase away the fear.

"I love you."

"I know." Moved by the desperation in his voice, she lifted a hand to his cheek. The urge to soothe and ease was still new to her. "We'll both get used to it eventually."

"Hello."

They drew apart to see Caroline standing in the doorway. Her dark, straight hair skimmed her shoulders. Beaded columns swung at her ears. There was a small smile on her face, a quietly lovely face that was animated by large, amused eyes. She was wearing a baggy man's shirt, trim denim pants and beaded moccasins. In her arms she held a gurgling baby.

"Mom." Sunny dashed across the room to hug both woman and child. She was taller than Caroline and had to bend slightly to give her the same enthusiastic kiss she had given her father. Laughing, she took the baby. Then, holding him above her head, she began to turn in a circle. "Hi, Sam! How's it going? Oh, you're getting so big!"

"He has his sister's appetite," Caroline pointed out.

Grinning, Sunny planted the giggling baby on her hip. "J.T., this is my mother, Caroline, and my brother, King Samuel."

"J.T." Caroline's artist's eyes had already seen the resemblance and made the connection. "You must be Cal's brother."

"Yes." The sense of unreality came back as she crossed the room. Rather than offering a hand, she kissed him.

"We were hoping we'd finally meet some of Cal's family. He's very proud of you."

"Is he?" A trace of resentment came through in his tone.

Caroline noticed it, let it pass. "Yes. Did your parents make the trip with you?"

"No. They weren't able to come."

"Oh." The disappointment in her eyes was brief but sincere. "Well, I hope we can get together one day. Where's Will?" she asked Sunny.

"Making tea."

"Of course. Please, sit down. You're an astrophysicist?"

"That's right." He settled back on the sofa, with Caroline Stone opposite him and Sunny on the floor with the baby.

"J.T.'s into time travel at the moment."

"Time travel?" Caroline smiled and crossed her slender legs. "Will'll go crazy. Though I think parallel universes are his current interest."

"What happened to reincarnation?"

"He's still a staunch disciple. He's convinced he was a member of the first Continental Congress."

"Always the revolutionary." Sunny tickled her brother's belly as she smiled up at Jacob. "My father likes to pick controversial subjects so he can argue about them. Oh, look! Sam's crawling!"

"A newly acquired skill." With two parts pride and one part wonder, Caroline watched her chubby, towheaded son pull himself across the rug. "Will's already taken a caseful of videos."

"I'm entitled," William said as he wheeled in a tea cart. "As I remember, Sunny went from crawl to walk to run so fast we hardly had time to blink."

"And you recorded it all on that secondhand movie camera." Caroline rose, stepped over her son, and kissed Will before she helped him with the tea.

"So…" William had already gone over his list of questions in the kitchen. "…did you just get into Portland?"

"This afternoon," Jacob told him, and accepted his cup of tea.

"You were looking for Cal when you tracked down Sunny."

"That's right." He sipped, trying to resolve himself to the fact that he was drinking Herbal Delight with the man who had invented it. "He'd given me the—" coordinates nearly slipped out "—directions to the cabin."

"The cabin?" The teacup paused on the way to William's lips. "You've been to the cabin—with Sunny?"

"We had a hell of a snowstorm last week." Sunny laid a hand lightly on her father's knee. "Lost power for a couple of days."

"Together?"

She managed to keep her expression bland. "It's hard to lose it separately in a space as small as the cabin."

Amused, Caroline watched her son crawl over Jacob's feet. "It's a shame you missed Cal and Libby. I hope you plan to wait until they get back."

The baby was chewing on his pant leg. After setting

his teacup aside, Jacob reached down to set Sam in his lap. "I'll wait."

"Where?" William wanted to know. Sunny dug her fingers into her father's knee.

"Did you know that J.T.'s experimenting with time travel?"

"Time travel?" Fascination warred with paternity. Paternity won. "Just how long were you two together in the mountains?"

Jacob let Sam gnaw on his index finger. "A couple of weeks."

"Really?" His eyes narrowed, and he laid a proprietary hand on Sunny's shoulder. "I suppose the snow kept you from making more suitable arrangements?"

Sunny rolled her eyes. Caroline sighed. Jacob ran a hand over Sam's fine, pale hair.

"The arrangement suited me well enough."

"I'll bet it did." William leaned forward, then hissed as Sunny dug again, shooting for the worn denim at his knees.

"Did you know, J.T., that my father absconded…" She liked the word, enjoyed rolling it off of her tongue. "…with my mother when she was sixteen?"

"Seventeen," William corrected.

"Not quite." This from Caroline as she sipped her tea.

He shot her a look. "You were only a couple months shy. And that was entirely different."

"Naturally," Sunny agreed.

"It was the times," William muttered. "It was the sixties."

Sunny kissed his sore knee. "That explains everything."

"You had to be there. Besides, we wouldn't have had to elope if Caro's father hadn't been so interfering and unreasonable."

"I'm sure you're right." Sunny fluttered her lashes at him. "There's nothing worse than a father who pokes his nose in where it doesn't belong."

He caught her nose between his two fingers and twisted. "Watch it."

She just grinned. "Tell me, is Granddad speaking to you yet?"

"Barely."

"Except when they make fools of themselves over Sam," Caroline put in. "He's almost forgiven us for the fact that you and Libby weren't around for him to spoil when you were babies. Would you like me to take Sam, J.T.?"

"No, he's fine." The baby was playing with Jacob's fingers, gurgling to them and sampling one occasionally. "He looks like you," he murmured, turning to Sunny.

Her lips curved. She couldn't have explained how it

made her feel to watch him cuddle a baby on his lap. "I like to think so."

William drummed his fingers on the arm of his chair. The Hornblower boys seemed to have some kind of charm that worked on his daughters. Though he'd decided Cal was nearly good enough for Libby, he was reserving judgment on this one.

"So, you're a scientist." William had a great deal of respect for scientists, but that didn't mean he was ready to accept the picture of his daughter snuggled up with one. In his cabin. Without any electricity.

"Yes."

Talkative son of a gun, William thought, and prodded deeper. "Astrophysics?"

"That's right."

"Where did you study?"

"Maybe you'd like his grade point average," Sunny muttered.

"Shut up." William patted her head. "I've always been fascinated with space, you see." This time his smile was cautiously friendly. "So I'm interested."

If this was the game, Jacob decided, he could play it. "I got my law degree from Princeton."

"Law?" Sunny said. "You never told me—"

"You didn't ask." His eyes dipped to her, then zeroed in on her father again. "Physics started out as a hobby."

"An unusual one," William mused.

"Yes." Jacob smiled. "Like growing herbs."

William had to laugh. "About time travel—"

"Take a break, Will," Caroline advised him. "You can grill the man more later. Your son needs to be changed."

"And it's my turn." William unfolded his long legs. He crossed to Jacob, his heart turning to mush as Sam lifted up his chubby arms. "There's my boy. Have some more tea," he told Jacob. "We'll talk about those experiments of yours later."

"I'll come with you." Sunny pushed herself up off the floor. "You can show me all the toys you bought him since last month."

"Wait till you see this train..." he said as they walked out.

"Will likes to pretend the toys are for Sam." Caroline smiled as she rose to fill Jacob's cup again. "I hope you're not too annoyed."

"By what?"

"The Spanish Inquisition." She moved back to sit on the arm of her chair. She reminded him of Sunny. "Actually, it was pretty mild, compared to what he put Cal through."

"Apparently Cal passed."

"We love him very much. Nothing would have made Will happier than to bring him into the business. But Cal has to fly, as I'm sure you know."

"He never wanted anything else."

"It shows. It was the same with Libby. She always knew what she wanted. It's more difficult for Sunny. I wonder sometimes if all that energy and intelligence hasn't given her too many choices. You'd understand that." At his questioning look, she continued. "From a law degree from Princeton to astrophysics. That's quite a leap."

With a brief turn at professional boxing in between. He shrugged. "It takes some of us longer to make up our minds."

"And those kind of people usually jump in with both feet. Sunny does."

She was subtler than her husband, Jacob thought, and more difficult to put off. "She's the most fascinating woman I've ever met."

And he is in love with her, Caroline reflected. Not happy about it, but in love. "Sunny's like a tapestry, woven in bold colors. Some of the threads are incredibly strong and durable. Others are impossibly delicate. The result is admirable. But a work of art needs love, as well as admiration." She lifted her hands. "She'd hate to know I described her that way."

His gaze shifted to the vivid, blending colors of the wall hanging. "She wouldn't care for the delicate."

"No." Caroline felt a tug of regret, and of relief. So he knew her younger daughter, and he understood her.

"It's old-fashioned, I suppose, but all Will and I really want is to know that she's happy."

"It's not old-fashioned." His mother had said almost the same words to him about Cal before he'd left home.

With a sigh, Caroline turned to glance at the wall hanging he was studying. "That's one of my older pieces. I made that while I was pregnant with Sunny. I sold most of my work back then, but for some reason I held on to this one."

"It's beautiful."

On impulse she rose to take it down from the wall. Her fingers slid over it. She remembered sitting at her handmade loom, watching the sunlight play on the colors as she chose them, blended them. With Will in the garden, Libby sleeping on a blanket spread on the grass and a child moving in her womb. The image was all the sweeter for the time that had passed between.

"I'd like you to have it."

If she had offered him a Rembrandt or an O'Keeffe, he would have been no more stunned. "I couldn't."

"Why not?"

"It's priceless."

She laughed at that. "Oh, my agent puts prices on my work. Ridiculous prices, for the most part. I'd hate to think that my pieces will only end up in art galleries or museums." She folded it. "It would mean a lot more if I knew some of them were being enjoyed by my family." When he said nothing, she held it out. "My daughter took your brother's name. That makes us family."

He didn't want to feel like family. He needed to hold on to his resentment, to go on thinking of Caroline and William Stone as names in history. But he found himself reaching out and taking the soft cloth.

"Thank you."

The nursery was painted a soft green. An antique iron crib in white was draped with a blanket Caroline had woven in pastels. The room was full of toys, many of which Sam would have no interest in for years. But there were dozens of stuffed animals, ranging from elephants to the traditional teddy bear.

Picking one up, Sunny waited until her father laid Sam on the changing table. "You're pathetic."

"Maybe you don't remember the punishment for sass," Will said mildly as he unsnapped Sam's overalls.

"I'm a little too big for you to make me sit in a chair until I apologize."

He shot her a look. "Don't bet on it."

"Dad." Sighing, she set the bear aside. "From the time I turned thirteen you've interrogated every male I've brought into the house."

"I like to know who my daughter's seeing socially. There's no crime in that."

"There is the way you do it."

Sam gurgled and kicked his feet as Will freed him of his diaper. Will dusted powder on him, enjoying the scent. "I liked you better when you were this size."

"Tough." She walked over to rest her elbow on his shoulder. Even at her most rebellious, she'd never been able to do anything but love him. "I suppose you're going to grill the girls Sam brings home when he starts dating."

"Of course. I'm not sexist." Neither was he stupid. "Do you want to tell me that you and J.T. have been spending a few platonic days in the cabin?"

"No."

"I didn't think so." He fastened a fresh diaper on his son. Life had been so simple, he thought, when all he'd had to worry about was diaper rash and teething. "Sunny, you haven't known the man more than a few weeks."

She stuck her tongue in her cheek. "Does this mean you've changed your views on free love?"

"The sexual revolution is over." He snapped Sam's overalls again. "For several very good reasons."

She held up a hand. "Before you start listing them, why don't I tell you I agree with you?"

That took some of the wind out of his sails. Sunny had come by her argumentative nature honestly. "Good. Then we understand each other."

"That promiscuity is neither morally nor ethically

correct nor physically wise? Absolutely. I've never been promiscuous."

"I'm relieved to hear it." Seeing Sam's eyes droop, Will took him to the crib. After winding up a mobile of circus animals, he laid his son down.

"I didn't say I was a virgin."

Will winced—he hated to think of himself as a fusty prude—then sighed. "I guess I suspected as much."

"Want to make me sit in a chair until I apologize?"

His lips quirked. "I don't think it would do much good at this point. It's not that I don't trust your judgment, Sunbeam."

She'd never been able to resist him. Moving closer, she took his face in her hands and kissed him. "But your judgment is so much better."

"Naturally." He grinned and patted her bottom. "It's one of the few advantages of hitting forty."

"You'll never be forty." She managed to keep her lips from curving. "Dad, I might as well confess. I have been with a man before."

"Not that weasely Carl Lommins."

She made a face. "Give me some credit. And don't interrupt—I'm making a point. When I was with someone it was because I was fond of him, because there was mutual respect and there was responsibility. You taught me that, you and Mom."

"So you're telling me I'm not supposed to worry about your relationship with J.T."

"No, I'm not telling you not to worry. But I am telling you I'm not fond of him."

"Well, then—"

"I'm in love with him."

He studied her eyes. When a man had been in love, passionately, with the same woman for most of his life, he recognized the signs. It was time to accept that he had seen those signs on his daughter's face the moment she had walked in the door.

"And?"

"And what?" she countered.

"What are you going to do about it?"

"I'm going to marry him." The statement surprised her enough to make her laugh. "He doesn't know it yet, because I just figured it out myself. When he goes back east, I'm going with him."

"And if he objects?"

Her chin came up. "He'll have to learn to live with it."

"I guess the problem is you're too much like me."

She put her arms around his neck to hug him close. "I won't like being so far away. But he's what I want."

"If he makes you happy." William drew her away. "He damn well better make you happy."

"I don't intend to give him a choice."

Chapter 10

"It'll be fun." Sunny navigated into a narrow parking space under a brightly lit sign that aggressively flashed Club Rendezvous. Jacob studied the winking colored lights with some doubt, and she patted his hand. "Trust me, pal, we need this."

"If you say so."

"I do. Besides, if I find out you can't dance, I want to be able to dump you now and save time." She just laughed when he twisted her ear. "And you owe me."

"Why is that?"

She flipped down the visor and gave what she could see of her face a quick check in the mirror. On impulse she pulled out a lipstick and painted her mouth a vivid red. "Because if I hadn't been so quick with the excuses you'd be eating dinner at my parents'."

"I liked your parents."

Touched, she leaned over to kiss his cheek. Seeing she'd left the imprint of her lips there, she rubbed at it with her thumb.

"Damn it."

"Hold still a minute," she complained when he backed away. "I've just about got it." Satisfied, she dropped the tube of lipstick back in her bag. "I know you like my parents. So do I. But you'd never have gotten nachos and margaritas at Will and Caro's." She lowered her voice. "My mother cooks."

Taking no chances, he rubbed at his cheek himself. "Is that a crime in this state?"

"She cooks things like alfalfa fondue."

"Oh." Once he'd managed to imagine it he'd decided he much preferred the spicy Mexican meal they had shared a short time before. "I guess I do owe you."

"Your very life," she agreed. Opening her door, she squeezed herself through the narrow opening between it and the neighboring car. The flashing lights danced over her, making her look exactly as she was—exciting and exotic. "And after a couple of weeks in nature's bosom I figure we could both use some live music—the louder the better—a rowdy crowd and some air clogged with cigarette smoke."

"Sounds like paradise." He managed, with some effort, to push himself out the other door. "Sunny, I don't feel right about you exchanging all your currency."

She lifted both brows, half amused, half puzzled, by his phrasing. "You exchange currency when you go into a foreign country. What I've been doing is called spending money."

"Whatever. I don't have any with me to spend."

She thought it was a pity that a man so obviously intelligent and dedicated should earn a small salary. "Don't worry about it." She'd only started counting pennies herself since she'd become self-supporting. So far, she hadn't shown much of a knack for it. "If I get to Philadelphia, you can pick up the tab."

"We'll talk about it later." He needed to change the subject, and he found the answer close at hand. "I wanted to ask you what you call that outfit you're wearing."

"This?" She glanced down at the snug, short and strapless red leather dress under her winter coat. "Sexy," she decided, running a tongue over her teeth. "What do you call it?"

"We'll talk about that later, too."

With her arm through his, she crossed the broken sidewalk. The swatch of formfitting leather didn't provide much protection against the wind, but it felt good to wear something other than jeans. It felt even better to note how often Jacob's gaze skimmed over her legs.

The cold was forgotten when she opened the door to a blast of heat and music.

"Ah…civilization."

He saw only a dim room dazzled by intermittent flashes of light. The music was every bit as loud as she'd promised, pulsing with bass, blaring with horns. He could smell smoke and liquor, sweat and perfume. Through it all was the constant din of voices and laughter.

While he took it in, she passed their coats to the checker on duty and slipped the stub in her bag.

She was right. He'd needed it—not just the sensory stimulation, not just the anonymous crowd, but also the firsthand look at twentieth-century socializing.

Overall there was very little difference from what he might have found in his own time. People, then and then, tended to gather together for their entertainment. They wanted music and company, food and drink. Times might change, but people's needs were basically the same.

"Come on." She was dragging him through the crowd to where tables were crammed together on two levels. On the first was a long bar. There was a man rather than a synthetic behind it, serving drink and setting out bowls filled with some kind of finger food. People crowded there, hip to hip.

On the second level was a half circle of stage where

the musicians performed. Jacob counted eight of them, in various kinds of dress, holding instruments that pitched a wall of sound that roared out of tall boxes on either corner of the stage.

In front of them, on a small square of floor, tangles of arms and legs and bodies twisted in various ways to the beat. He noted the costumes they chose and saw that there was no standard. Snug pants and baggy ones, long skirts and brief ones, vivid colors and unrelieved black. Women wore shoes flat to the floor or, like Sunny, shoes with slender spikes at the back.

He imagined this meant those particular women wanted to be taller. But it had the side effect of making it very pleasant to look at their legs.

He appreciated the style of nonconformity, the healthy expression of individual tastes. He knew there had been a space of time between this and his own when society in general had accepted a uniform. A brief period, Jacob mused, but it must have been a miserably dull one.

As he stood and observed, waitresses in short skirts bustled on both levels, balancing trays and scribbling the orders shouted at them.

Inefficient, he thought, but interesting. It was simpler to press a button on an order box and receive your requirements from a speedy droid. But it was a bit friendlier this way.

With her hand in his, Sunny led him up a short flight of curving stairs and began to scout around for an empty table. "I forgot it was Saturday night," she shouted at him. "It's always a madhouse on Saturdays."

"Why?"

"Date night, pal," she said, and laughed. "Don't worry, we'll squeeze in somewhere." But she abandoned her search to smile at him. "What do you think?"

He lifted a hand to toy with the trio of balls that hung from slender chains at her ears. "I like it."

"The Marauders are good. The band." She gestured as the sax player went into a screaming solo. "They're very hot out here."

"In here," he corrected. "It's hot in here."

"No, I mean… Never mind." Someone bumped her from behind. Taking it in stride, she wound her arms around Jacob's neck. "I guess this is our first date."

He ignored the crowd and kissed her. "How's it going so far?"

"Just dandy."

Taking that to mean "good," he kissed her again. Her satisfied sigh set off a chain reaction inside him. "We could always just stand here," he said, directly in her ear. "I don't think anyone would notice."

"You were right," she said on another sigh. "It is hot in here. Maybe we should just—"

"Sunny!" Someone caught her by the waist, spun her

around and, ending on a dip, pressed a hard, wet kiss to her mouth. "Baby, you're back."

"Marco."

"What's left of me. I've been pining away for weeks." He slung a friendly arm around her shoulders. "Where'd you disappear to?"

"The mountains." She smiled, pleased to see him. He was skinny, unpretentious and harmless. Despite the dramatic kiss, they had decided years before not to complicate their friendship with romance. "How's the real world?"

"Dog-eat-dog, love. Thank God." He glanced over her shoulder and found himself being burned alive by a pair of direct green eyes. "Ah...who's your friend?"

"J.T." She laid a hand on Jacob's arm. "This is Marco, an old poker buddy. You don't want to play with J.T., Marco. He's murder."

Marco didn't have to be told twice. "How ya doing?" He didn't offer his hand, because he wanted to keep it.

"All right." Jacob measured him. He figured if the man kissed Sunny again it would be simple enough to break his skinny neck.

"J.T. happens to be the brother of my sister's husband."

"Small world."

Jacob didn't bat an eye. "Smaller than you think."

"Right." If Marco had been wearing a tie he would

have loosened it. But with his collar already open he didn't have a clue how to ease the constriction in his throat. "Listen, do you guys need a table?"

"Absolutely."

"We pulled some together back there, if you want to climb in."

"Okay." She looked up at Jacob. "Okay?"

"Sure." He was already annoyed with himself. The jealousy had been an emotional rather than an intellectual reaction. He watched Sunny's long legs as she walked between the tables. And an entirely justified reaction. Maybe men had progressed, but they had always been, would always be, territorial.

Half a dozen people greeted Sunny by name as they stopped at the table. Because most of the introductions were lost in the roar of the music, Jacob only nodded as he took his seat.

"This round's on me," Marco announced when he finally managed to flag down a waitress. "Same thing," he told her. "Plus a glass of chardonnay for the lady and…" He lifted a brow at Jacob.

"A beer. Thanks."

"No problem. I sold three cars today."

"Good for you." Sunny leaned over a bit, easily pitching her voice above the noise as she elaborated for Jacob's benefit. "Marco's a car dealer."

Jacob got the image of Marco shuffling automobiles,

then passing them around a poker table. "Congratulations" seemed the safest possible comment.

"I do okay. Just let me know if you're in the market. We got in a shipment of real honeys this week."

Jacob spared a glance at the brunette on his other side as she rubbed her arm against his. "I'll do that."

Relieved that Sunny's new friend no longer looked as though he wanted to rearrange his face, Marco shifted his chair a little closer. "So what do you drive, J.T.?"

There was a universal moan around the table. Marco accepted it with a good-natured shrug and popped a handful of peanuts into his mouth.

"Hey, it's my job."

"Like taking little old ladies for test drives is a job," someone joked.

"It's a living." Marco grinned. "None of us are rocket scientists."

"J.T. is," Sunny said.

"Are you?" The brunette scooted her chair closer.

She had big brown eyes, Jacob noted. Eyes that just brimmed with invitations. "In a manner of speaking."

"Oh, I just love brainy men."

Amused, Jacob picked up the beer the waitress set in front of him. He caught the look Sunny shot across the table. He recognized it. Jealousy, it appeared, was contagious. Nothing could have pleased him more. He took a long swig and tolerated the smoke the brunette blew in his direction. It was no use telling her that she was endangering her very attractively packaged lungs.

"Do you?"

She kept her eyes on his as she slowly crushed out the cigarette. "Oh, yes. I'm very attracted to intelligence."

"Let's dance." Sunny shoved back her chair and snagged Jacob's sleeve. "Nice try, Sheila," she muttered, and dragged Jacob onto the dance floor.

"Is that her name? Sheila?"

She turned to him, into him, and tilted her chin upward. "Who wants to know?"

"Don't you want me to be nice to your friends?" He settled his hands on her hips. With her heels, her eyes were level with his. And her body fit his perfectly.

"No." Her mouth moved into a pout as she twined her arms around his neck. "At least not the stacked ones."

Curious, he looked back at the table. "Is she stacked?"

"As if you didn't notice. Unfortunately, her I.Q. measures the same as her bustline."

"I like your...I.Q. better."

"Good thinking." Grinning, she brushed a kiss over his mouth. "I can't blame her for giving it her best shot. You're awfully cute."

"Small dogs are cute," he muttered. "Babies are cute."

"You like babies."

"Yes, why not?"

She toyed with the ends of his hair. "Just checking. Anyway, you are cute. And sexy." She took a playful nip at his bottom lip. "And bi..... She settled her cheek against his as he drew her closer. And mine, she thought. All mine. "What does the *T* stand for?" she murmured.

"Which *T*?"

"In J.T."

"Nothing."

"It has to stand for something." She let out a sound of pleasure. "You dance very well." The sax was playing again, crying the blues this time. Sunny's eyes dipped closed as Jacob molded her against him. They were hardly moving in the press of bodies surrounding them. As his hands roamed over her back and his lips down her throat she didn't care if they ever moved again.

Her thighs brushed against his. The leather fitted her like a second skin, one he was already imagining peeling away from her. As he turned her in his arms, slowly, sinuously, he shifted to taste the bare flesh of her shoulder. Even over the echoing music he could hear her skin humming. Lazily he trailed his lips back to toy with hers.

"You smell incredible. Like spring in the desert, hot, with some lingering trace of flowers gone wild."

Unable to resist, she deepened the kiss until her head swam. "J.T.?"

"Yes?"

"I'm not sure, but I think we could get arrested for this."

"It would be worth it."

She opened her eyes, met his. "Let's go home. I don't like crowds the way I used to."

They stayed a week, so that she could drag him to movies, malls, more clubs. She attributed his constant fascination to the fact that he'd never been in the North-west before. Each time they went out, it was as though he were seeing things for the first time. Because of that, she enjoyed the hours and the errands more than she ever had.

When they were alone, when she trembled in his arms, she realized that it didn't matter where they were. They were together. And if with each passing moment she fell more deeply in love, she did so freely and with absolute joy.

For the first time in her life she began to think of a future with a man, one man. She imagined passing through the years with him—not always content, but always satisfied. She thought of a home, and if white picket fences and car pools didn't enter the fantasy, chil-dren did. She could picture the arguments, the noise and the laughter.

Before much longer, she thought, they would talk about it. They would plan.

He allowed himself the week. A handful of days meant so little in the vastness of time. And meant so much to him. He recorded everything he could, and branded the rest on his memory. He didn't mean to forget, not an instant.

Yet he worried about how he could tell her where he had to travel when he left her so that it would hurt the least. More, he worried because he was no longer sure he had the courage to live without her.

When they left to go back to the cabin he told himself that it was the beginning of the end. If it had to end—and he saw no alternative—it would end honestly. He would tell her everything.

"You're so quiet," she said as they turned up the long, bumpy road that led to the cabin.

"I was thinking."

"Well, that's fine, but you haven't picked one fight in five hours. I'm worried about you."

"I don't want to fight with you."

"Now I'm really worried." She'd known that something was on his mind, something that caused her palms to sweat. Deliberately she made her voice light and cheerful. "We'll be back in a few minutes. Once you're trapped inside the cabin, hauling wood and eating out of a can, you'll be your old cranky self."

"Sunny, we have to talk."

She moistened her lips. "All right." Her nerves began to hum as she stopped the car in front of the cabin. "Before or after we unload?"

"Now." It had to be now. He took her hand and said the first words that came to mind. "I love you so much."

The little fist of fear in her stomach unclenched. "We're never going to fight if you keep talking like that." She shifted closer to kiss his cheek. It was then that she noticed the smoke pumping out of the chimney. "Jacob, someone's here."

"What?"

"In the cabin." She saw the front door open. "Libby!" With a laugh, she shoved the car door open and bounded out. "Libby, you scared me to death." As Jacob watched, she threw her arms around a slim brunette. "Look at you! You're so tanned!"

"There's a lot of sun in Bora Bora." Libby kissed her sister's cheeks. "When we got back last night we thought you'd skipped out on us."

"Just a quick trip into the real world to recharge."

Libby's laugh was smooth and easy. She knew her sister very well. "That's what I told Cal. All your books were still here." Suddenly she gripped both of Sunny's hands. "Oh, Sunny, I'm so glad you're back. I can't wait to tell you. I—" A movement caught her eye. Glancing over, she saw Jacob as he climbed out of the Land

Rover. As their eyes met, her half smile of greeting faded and her fingers tightened on Sunny's.

"What? What is it? Oh." Smiling, Sunny turned. "Guess who dropped in? This is Jacob, Cal's brother."

"I know." Libby felt as though the ground had vanished from under her feet. She'd seen his face before, in the picture Cal had kept on his ship. But this was no picture. It was a flesh-and-blood man, a furious one. As they stared at each other in silence, the blood seeped slowly out of her face.

He's come for Cal, she thought, and had to bite back the scream of protest that rose into her throat.

She's terrified, he realized. Something moved inside him that he stubbornly ignored. He wouldn't feel for her. He wouldn't think of her as anything but the obstacle preventing his brother from returning home.

"J.T.?" Instinctively Sunny put a protective arm around Libby's shoulders. There was something here, she realized. And she was the only one not in on the secret. "Libby, you're shivering. You shouldn't be standing out here without a coat. Let's go inside." She tossed a look back over her shoulder. "Let's all go inside."

"I'm all right." Shaken, Libby walked inside to the fire and tried to warm her icy hands. No amount of heat could warm her trembling heart. She wouldn't look at him again, not until she had herself under some kind of control. In the back of her mind, the little germ of fear had lived. Someday they would come for him. But she hadn't believed it would be so soon. They'd had so little time.

Time, she thought bitterly. It was a word she could learn to hate.

Sunny stood between them, baffled. The tension was so thick in the small room that she could smell it as easily as the woodsmoke. "All right." She looked from Libby's rigid back to Jacob's stony face without any idea who she should go to. "Would either of you like to tell me what's going on?"

"Hey, Libby, if that was that sexy sister of yours, I want to tell her—"

Barefoot, his sweatshirt torn, Cal strode in from the kitchen. Everyone turned toward him. It was like a slow, deliberate ballet. His easy grin froze. All motion stopped.

"J.T." His voice was hardly more than a whisper as joy and disbelief flooded through him. "J.T.," he said again. Then, with a whoop, he was across the room, grabbing his brother in a hard hug. "Oh, God, Jacob! It's really you!"

Libby watched them until tears blurred her vision and she turned away.

Sunny beamed. The two brothers held each other in a fierce embrace. She could see the emotions run over Jacob's face and found them beautiful.

"I can't believe it," Cal murmured, pulling his brother back to study, to devour, his face. "You're really here. How?"

He kept his hands on Cal's arms, needing the simple and tangible contact. "The same way as you, but with more finesse. You look good." Somehow he'd expected to find Cal pale and thin and tired from coping with the twentieth century. Instead, his brother was tanned, alert and obviously happy.

"You, too." His smile faded a bit. "Mom? Dad?"

"They're fine."

Cal nodded. It was a hurt he had learned to live with. "You got my message. I couldn't be sure."

"We received it," Jacob said dully.

"You've met Libby, then." Regret vanished. Turning, he held a hand out for his wife. She didn't move.

"We've met." Jacob inclined his head and waited. She could take the first step.

"You'll both have a lot to talk about." Using every ounce of effort, she managed to keep her voice steady.

"Libby." Her name was a murmur as Cal crossed to her. He laid a hand on her cheek until she lifted her eyes to his. He saw the love and the fear in them. "Don't."

"I'm fine." Calling up more strength, she squeezed his hand. "I have some things to do upstairs. You two should catch up." She shifted her glance to Jacob. "I know you've missed each other."

Turning, she fled up the stairs.

Sunny shifted her gaze from her sister's retreating back to Cal's unsmiling face and then to Jacob's angry eyes. "What the hell is going on here?"

"Go up with her, will you?" Cal laid a hand on her shoulder but continued to look after his wife. "I don't want her to be alone."

"All right." She could already see, just by looking at the two of them, that she'd get no explanations here. She'd damn well get one from Libby.

Cal waited until Sunny had climbed the stairs. Facing his brother again, he recognized the fury, the passion, and the hurt in him. "We have to talk."

"Yes."

"Not here." He thought of his wife.

"No." Jacob thought of Sunny. "We'll go to my ship."

Sunny paused outside the bedroom door. Taking a deep breath, she pushed it open. Libby sat on the edge of the bed, hands folded. There were no tears. Tears would have been less heartbreaking than the despair on her face.

"Honey, what is it?"

Libby felt as though she were in a dream. Looking up, she focused on the reality of her sister. "How long has he been here?"

"About three weeks." Sunny sat on the bed to take

Libby's hand in hers. "Talk to me. I thought you'd be happy to finally meet Cal's brother."

"I am—for him." Hoping that much was true, she pressed a hand to her jittery stomach. "Did he explain to you why he's here? Where he's from?"

"Of course." Puzzled, Sunny gave her a little shake. "Come on, Libby, snap out of it. J.T.'s a little rough around the edges, but he isn't a monster. He's just concerned about Cal, and maybe a little hurt that he chose you and settled here."

"Oh, God." Unable to sit, Libby rose to pace to the window. She heard the hum of an engine and saw the Land Rover disappear into the forest. "I would have let him go," she said quietly, and closed her eyes. "Back then I was prepared to. I couldn't have asked him to give up his family, his life. But now I can't let him go. I won't."

"Where would he go?"

Libby rested her head on the cool glass of the window. "Back." She laughed a little. "Forward. Jacob must have told you how impossibly complicated it all is."

Rising, Sunny walked over to lay her hands on Libby's shoulders. They were taut, like bundles of wire. Automatically she worked to relax them. "Cal's a grown man, Libby, and staying here was his choice. J.T.'s just going to have to accept that."

"But will he?"

"When he first got here, J.T. was angry and resentful. He just wasn't able to understand Cal's feelings. But things have changed. For both of us."

Slowly Libby turned. What was in her sister's heart was clearly written in her eyes. Libby felt a lurch of panic. "Oh, Sunny."

"Hey, don't look at me like that." She grinned. "I'm in love, not terminally ill."

"But what are you going to do?"

"I'm going to go back with him."

With an inarticulate cry, Libby threw her arms around Sunny's neck. She clung, rocking.

"For Lord's sake, Libby, you're as bad as Jacob. It's only Philadelphia. You're acting like I'm going to set up housekeeping on Pluto."

"There aren't any settled colonies on Pluto."

With a strangled laugh, Sunny pulled away. "Well, I guess that leaves that out. We'll have to make do with a condo in Philly."

Libby studied Sunny's face, and her expression gradually changed. The tears that had dampened her eyes dried. "You don't understand, do you?"

"I understand that I love J.T. and he loves me. We haven't talked about life commitments yet, but it's only a matter of time." She stopped, wary. "Libby, why are you looking at me as though you want to wring my neck?"

"Not yours." Libby's voice had firmed. She might be the quieter of the two, but when those she loved were threatened she could put an Amazon queen to shame. "The bastard."

"I beg your pardon?"

"I said he's a bastard."

Sisterly love notwithstanding, Sunny's hackles were rising. "Now look, Libby—"

She shook her head. She wasn't about to be stopped now. "Did he tell you he loved you?"

Nearly out of patience, Sunny snapped off an oath. Then: "Yes."

"And you've gone to bed with him."

Sunny's eyes narrowed. "Have you been taking lessons from Dad?"

"Of course you've gone to bed with him," Libby muttered, pacing the room. "He's made you fall in love with him, taken you to bed, and hasn't had the decency to tell you."

Sunny's foot was tapping a rapid tattoo. "Tell me what?"

"That he and Cal are from the twenty-third century."

Sunny's foot stopped. In the sudden silence, she gaped at Libby. All that sun, she thought. Her poor sister had had her brain fried in Bora Bora. Slowly she crossed the room.

"Lib, I want you to lie down while I get you a cold cloth."

"No." Still fueled by fury, Libby shook her head. "You sit down while I go get you a brandy. Trust me. You're going to need it."

When Cal stepped onto the bridge of the ship, the wave of nostalgia rolled over him like warm water. The cargo planes he piloted in the life he'd chosen satisfied his need to fly, but they weren't much of a challenge. Unable to resist, he ran his hands over the command console.

"She's a beauty, J.T. New model?"

"Yes, I thought it best to have it designed specifically for this trip. We made some adjustments for heat and maneuverability."

Cal couldn't prevent his hand from gripping the throttle. "I'd like to take her up, see what she can do."

"Be my guest."

Cal laughed. "We'd be spotted in the first thousand miles and find ourselves on the front page of the *National Enquirer*."

"Which is?"

"You have to see some things for yourself." Reluctantly he turned away from the console and temptation. Again he studied Jacob's face, feature by feature. "God, it's good to see you."

"How could you do it, Cal?"

Blowing out a long breath, he sat in the pilot's chair. "It's a long story."

"I read the report."

Cal gave him a long, steady look. "Some things don't come through in reports. You've seen her."

"Yes, I've seen her."

"I love her, J.T. I couldn't begin to tell you how much."

Jacob felt a spark of empathy and banked it down. He couldn't think of Sunny now. "We thought you were dead. Almost six months."

"I'm sorry."

"Are you?" Jacob swung to the viewscreen to stare out at the snow. "Five months and twenty-three days after you were reported lost, your ship crash landed about sixty kilometers from the McDowell base in the Baja. Empty. We had your reports." His gaze flashed back to his brother. "And I had to watch Mom and Dad grieve all over again."

"I wanted you to know where I was. And why. J.T., I didn't plan this. You saw the log."

"I saw it." His jaw set. "You should be dead. I calculated the probability factor of you pulling out of that void in one piece. There was none." For the first time he smiled. "You've always been a hell of a pilot, Cal."

"Yeah, but you can't input fate into computer banks."

He'd thought about that long and hard over the past months. "I was meant for Libby, J.T. You can calculate into the next millennium and that won't change. As much as I love you, I can't leave her and go back."

In silence, J.T. studied him. He hated most of all that he understood. Weeks before, only weeks, he would have argued, shouted. He would have locked Cal in a cabin and taken off for home without giving him a choice. "Does she love you as much?"

A ghost of a smile played on Cal's lips. "She never asked me to stay. In fact, she did everything she could to help me prepare for the return trip. She even asked to go with me. She would have given up everything."

"Instead, you stayed here. You gave up everything."

"Do you think it was easy for me to make the choice?" Cal demanded. He pushed himself out of the chair, driven by fury and frustration. "It was the hardest thing I've ever done. Damn it, there was no choice. I didn't know if the ship would make it back, and I couldn't risk her life. I was prepared to risk my own, but not hers. If I had left her, I would have been right back in the void again. And I wouldn't have cared."

Jacob didn't want to understand. But he did. "I've spent two years working on perfecting this time-travel procedure, having this ship designed, fine-tuning all the equations. I'm not saying that more work, more study, isn't necessary, but I made it without any major problems. The success factor is 88.57. Come home, Cal, and bring her with you."

Cal stared at the viewscreen. He'd learned a great deal over the past year. The most important lesson was that life was not simple. The choices to be made could not be made lightly.

"There's another piece of data you haven't considered, J.T. Libby's pregnant."

Chapter 11

She didn't speak. In the past thirty minutes, Sunny had gone from believing her sister had a wicked case of sunstroke to wondering if she herself had gone quietly mad without noticing it.

The twenty-third century. Black holes. Spaceships. Sunny had finally lapsed into silence as Libby had recounted a story about a mission to Mars—dear Lord, Mars—and Cal's fateful encounter with an uncharted black hole, which, through a combination of luck, skill and the mysterious hand of destiny, had shot him backward from the middle of the twenty-third century to the spring of last year.

The confused Cal, an intergalactic cargo pilot with an affection for flying and poetry, had become a time traveler.

Time travel.

Oh, God, she thought. *Time travel.*

She remembered clearly the faint smile on Jacob's face when he had told her of his current experiments. But that didn't mean— No. She took a steadying breath, determined to control her wandering imagination.

It had to be some sort of joke. People did not, accidentally or otherwise, zoom through time and fall in love. Jacob was from Philadelphia, she reminded herself as she gulped down brandy. He was a scientist with a bad attitude, and that was all.

"You don't believe me," Libby said with a sigh.

Care and patience, Sunny told herself as she dragged a hand through her hair. Her sister needed care and patience. "Honey, let's just take this slow."

"You think I'm making it up."

"I'm not sure what I think." She took a cleansing breath. "Okay, you're trying to tell me that Cal, a former captain in—what was it?"

"The International Space Force."

"Right. That he crashed his spaceship in the forest, after being sent through time by an encounter with a black hole."

She'd hoped that when she said it herself, when Libby heard it repeated, her sister would come out of whatever spell she was in. But Libby just nodded. "That's fairly accurate."

"Fairly accurate." Sunny tried again. "And now Jacob, going about it through more organized methods, followed the same route so he could visit with his brother."

"He wants to take him back. I could see it by the way he looked at me."

The misery on Libby's face had Sunny reaching out a hand. "Cal loves you. Nothing J.T. did or didn't do could change that."

"No, but…Sunny, can't you see? He didn't pop up here on impulse. He must have worked for months, even years, to find the way. If a man's obsessed with something—"

"All right," she interrupted. "He didn't pop up here on impulse. For reasons I've never fully understood, he's angry that Cal married you and decided to live in Oregon."

"Not just Oregon," Libby shot back. "Twentieth-century Oregon."

"Now, take it slow, honey. I know you're upset, but—"

"Upset?" Libby countered. "Damn right I'm upset. The man traveled over two hundred years, and he's not going to want to go back without Cal."

At a loss, Sunny flopped back on the bed. "Libby, you've got to get ahold of yourself. You're the sensible one, remember? You have to know this is all nonsense."

"Okay." Deciding on a different tack, she took a deep breath. "Can you tell me, honestly tell me, that you haven't noticed something odd about J.T.?" She held up a hand before Sunny could answer. "Not just eccentric, not just endearingly different, but downright odd?"

"Well, I…"

"Ah." Taking her sister's hesitation for agreement, she pressed on. "How did he get here?"

"I don't know what you mean."

"I mean…did he drive up in a car? I didn't notice one."

"No, he didn't come in a car. At least…" She rubbed her suddenly damp hands on her thighs. "He walked out of the woods."

"Walked out of the woods." Libby nodded grimly. "In the middle of winter."

"Lib, I'll concede that J.T.'s a little unusual."

"The way he seems fascinated or puzzled by ordinary objects?"

She remembered the kitchen faucet. "Well, yes."

"The way he doesn't always understand colloquialisms or phrases?"

"That, too, but—Libby, just because the man acts a little odd occasionally and has a hard time with slang doesn't mean he's an alien from outer space."

"Not an alien," Libby said patiently. "He's as human as you or I. He's just from the twenty-third century."

"Oh, is that all?"

"Maybe there's a simpler way to convince you." She rose and took Sunny's hand. "Whatever happens between Cal and me, we'll work it out together. But you have to understand it, all of it. I'm only doing this because you have a right to know what you're walking into."

She nodded. She didn't dare speak, because too much of what Libby had told her made a horrible kind of sense. And she was afraid, very afraid.

With competent movements, Libby took what seemed to be a watch from the deep drawer of her desk. While Sunny looked on, she attached a line of clear wire from the stem of the watch to the computer. After booting up the machine, she gestured.

"Come on over."

Cautious, Sunny joined her. "What is that thing?"

"It's Cal's wrist unit. Computer."

Working.

Sunny jumped back a foot at the sound of the mechanical voice and sent a chair tumbling. "How did you do that?"

"With a mix of twentieth-century and twenty-third-century technology."

"But...but...but..."

"You haven't seen anything yet," Libby warned, and

faced the screen again. "Computer, relate file information on Jacob Hornblower."

Hornblower, Jacob, born Philadelphia, June 12, 2224. Astrophysicist, currently head of AP department at Durnam Science Laboratory, Philadelphia. Graduated Princeton University magna cum laude 2242, earned degree in law 2244. Status AAA. Doctorate in astrophysics from O'Bannion 2248. Named MVP Intergalactic Softball League 2247-49. Position: pitcher. ERA 1.28.

Sunny bit back a hysterical giggle. "Stop."

The computer went silent. On rubbery legs, Sunny stepped back until she collided with the bed.

"It's true, isn't it?"

"Yes. Take a few deep breaths," Libby advised her. "It takes a while to absorb it."

"He told me he was experimenting with time travel." She felt the laughter bubble up again, hot and uncontrollable. "That's a good one." She squeezed her eyes shut. It was a dream, she told herself, just a ridiculous dream. But when she opened her eyes again everything was the same. "Looks like the joke's on me." She heard the door slam on the floor below. Instantly she was on her feet. "I'm going to have this out with him, right now."

"Why don't you—" Libby cut herself off when Sunny rounded on her. "Never mind." She sunk back on the bed as Sunny charged down the stairs.

But it was Cal she ran into, not Jacob. "Where is he?" she demanded.

"He's, ah…out. Is Libby upstairs?"

"Yes." Feet spread, eyes challenging, she blocked the stairs. "She's upset."

"She needn't be."

Because what she saw in his eyes answered some of her questions, she relaxed. "I'm glad you realize what a lucky jerk you are, Caleb."

"I love you, too."

She relented enough to kiss him. Later, she decided. Later she would think all this through. And probably go insane. But for now she had a job to do.

"I want to know where your creep of a brother is. And don't try to put me off. Libby told me."

But he was still cautious. "Told you what?"

She tilted her head. "Is it too late to welcome you to the twentieth century?"

A new smile tugged at his mouth. "No. J.T.'s out in his ship. It's about five kilometers northeast. Just follow the tracks." He caught her arm before she could rush off. "He's going through a bad time, Sunny. I've hurt him."

"Not nearly as much as I'm going to."

He started to speak again, but he remembered that Jacob had always been able to take care of himself. He went upstairs to his wife.

She was still sitting on the bed, staring at, but not out of, the window. Her face was composed, her hands folded in her lap so that they pressed lightly against the life growing in her. Looking at her, Caleb felt a single stunning wave of love.

"Hi."

She jolted, struggled to smile. "Hi. Busy day." Before he could speak, she sprang up. "I've got a dozen things to do. I haven't finished unpacking, and I really ought to fix something special for dinner tonight."

"Wait a minute." He took her arms before she could walk by, then simply brought her into his. "I love you, Libby."

"I know." With her head on his shoulder, she held on.

"No, I don't think you do." Gently he pulled her away to study her face. "Even after all this time, I don't think you do. How could you think I would leave? Then or now."

She just shook her head.

"Sit down," he murmured.

"Caleb, I don't know what to say to you." She sat, twining her nervous fingers together. "I can only imagine how you must feel, having your brother here when you thought you'd never see him again. Being reminded of everything you gave up, and the people you left behind."

"Are you finished?"

Her only answer was a miserable shrug.

"J.T. gave me a copy of a letter he found when he dug up our time capsule." He pulled her fingers apart to link them with his as he sat beside her. "He didn't read it," he continued. "It was still in the envelope."

"How did he copy it if it was still in—" She caught herself and managed a small laugh. "Stupid question."

"You put it in the capsule so I'd be able to read it when I got back." He took it out of his pocket. Libby frowned at it. It looked precisely as it had when she'd slipped it into the box. And yet…the paper was different, she realized when she touched it. Thicker, stronger. And, she added to herself, probably not paper at all. At least not as she thought of paper.

"I stopped on the way back from the ship to read it." He spread the letter in his lap. "If I had been crazy enough to leave you, this would have brought me back. Somehow."

"It wasn't meant to do that."

"I know." He took her hand, kissed it. "What it means is a great deal to me. Do you remember what you wrote?"

"Some of it."

"This part." He looked down at the letter. "'I wanted you to know that in my heart I wanted you to be where you belonged.'" He set the letter aside. "Did you mean that?"

"Yes."

"Then you'll be happy to know that I'm exactly where I belong." With long, slow kisses, he eased her back on the bed. "And so are you."

Sunny didn't have any trouble finding the tracks. There were only two sets, both from the Land Rover. One leading away from the cabin and one leading back. Her face grim, she kept her hands firm on the wheel and her mind empty.

She wouldn't think, not yet. Once she had begun to think it would probably send her screaming off a cliff. True, she'd always had an affection for the unusual, but this…this was going a bit too far.

When she saw the ship, nestled comfortably on a blanket of snow, she hit the brakes too hard and sent the Land Rover skidding sideways. It looked as big as a house.

She imagined it was half the size of the cargo ship Cal had piloted. Probably sleeker, jazzier. Its smooth white finish gleamed in the sunlight. She saw what appeared to be a window that banded around the bow. As she gaped, Jacob stepped up to it and looked out at her.

The sight of him inside it, inside of something that shouldn't even exist, turned her blank astonishment back into fury. Abandoning the Land Rover, she leaped out and stormed over to the ship.

He released the hatch. The door slid silently open, and a set of stairs flowed out. She mounted them, moving a little slower now. Going over the speech he'd planned, Jacob reached out to take her hand and help her through the entranceway.

"Sunny, I—" Whatever he had planned to say was interrupted when her fisted hand connected solidly with his jaw. Off balance and seeing stars, he stumbled back and landed hard on the deck.

She loomed over him, righteous fury glowing in her eyes. "Get up, you miserable coward, so I can hit you again."

He sat where he was for a moment, rubbing a hand over his jaw. He didn't mind the blow so much. He knew he'd had it coming. But he didn't care to be called a coward. Under the circumstances, though, it was best to let her get it all out of her system.

"You're upset."

"Upset?" The word hissed out between her teeth. "I'll show you upset." Because he obviously wasn't going to get up, she dived onto him.

She knocked the wind out of him with another punch as he grappled for her hands. "Damn it, Sunny, stop. I'm going to have to hurt you."

"Hurt me?" Blind with anger, she struck out as he struggled to roll on top of her. This time her knee slipped by his guard and landed dead on. As the air whistled out of his lungs, he collapsed on top of her. "Get off me, you creep."

He couldn't have moved if his life had depended on it. The pain, deserved or not, was like a silvery shimmer from crotch to brain. His only defense was his weight as he sprawled breathlessly over her.

"Sunny…" He dragged air into his lungs and saw a new constellation. "Your match," he conceded.

The fight had drained out of her. She didn't want him to know how weak and helpless she felt. With her jaw tensed, she prayed her voice wouldn't tremble.

"I said get off me."

"As soon as I'm sure I'm still intact. If you let me get my wind back, we can go another round." He managed to lift his head.

She was crying. Huge, silent tears welled up in her eyes and slid down her cheeks. More stunned by them than by the blow, he shook his head. "Don't." He brushed the tears away, but more fell to replace them. "Damn it, Sunny, stop it."

"Let go of me."

He rolled aside, determined to leave her alone until she composed herself. Before he realized it, he was gathering her close, dragging her onto his lap, stroking her hair.

"Don't touch me." Her body was rigid. Anger and

humiliation battled inside her. "I don't want you to touch me."

"I know. I have to."

"You lied to me."

"Yeah." He pressed his lips to her hair. "I'm sorry."

"You used me."

"No." His arms tightened. "No. You know better than that."

"I don't know you at all." She tried to arch away, but he only cradled her closer. Abruptly she threw her arms around him, burying her face against his throat. "I hate you. I'll hate you as long as I live."

The tears were no longer silent. They poured out in hard, racking sobs as she clung to him. He said nothing, had nothing to say. The woman who had knocked him flat with a right hook he understood. The one who clawed and spit and fought he knew how to handle. This one, this soft, weeping bundle in his arms, was a mystery. Defenseless, heartbroken, fragile.

And he fell in love with this Sunny, as well.

She clung to him, hating herself. She wanted to strike out, to make him pay for breaking her heart, but she could only hold on, taking the comfort he offered.

Carefully he rose with her in his arms. He needed to soothe, to protect, to love. He wanted to stroke her until her tears dried, hold her until her body calmed again. Most of all he wanted to show her that of all the things he'd done falling in love with her was the most important.

She couldn't stop, though she despised every tear. She couldn't fight him now, at her weakest point. Now she could only hold on to him, let the storm rage and find some small comfort in the gentle way he held her.

He took her into his cabin, where the light was dim. The bed was water-soft, covered with pale blue sheets. The walls were blue, as well. A quiet, restful color. Still holding her, he lay with her on the bed while her tears dampened his cheek.

When her sobs began to lessen, he trailed his lips down her temple to her mouth. Her lips were wet, and they were still trembling. As his touched them, she pulled away to roll onto her side.

"Sunny." Feeling awkward, he touched her shoulder. "Please, talk to me."

She didn't bother to jerk his hand away. She just stared at the pale blue wall. "I feel like such a fool. Crying over you."

He didn't know if any woman had ever done that before. Certainly none had ever cried in his arms. "I never wanted to hurt you."

"Being lied to always hurts."

"I didn't lie. I just didn't tell you the truth." He could see the logic of it, needed to. But he doubted she could. "I was going to tell you everything today."

She nearly laughed. "Do they still use that old chestnut in the twenty-third century?" She had said it out loud. The twenty-third century. And she was in what could only be called a spaceship with a man who wouldn't be born until she was long dead. She'd have preferred to believe it was all a dream, but the pain was too real.

"I came for my brother," he told her. "I never planned to become involved with you, to fall in love with you. It happened too fast."

"I was there, remember?"

"Look at me."

She shook her head. "Let's just forget it, J.T. A man like you probably thinks he's entitled to have a woman in every century."

"I said look at me." Patience gone, he pulled her back, holding her by the shoulders so that she was forced to meet his eyes. "I love you."

The words seeped into her and weakened her resolve. Her only defense was heat. "Apparently the definition of love has changed. Don't lose any sleep over it. I'll be fine."

"Will you listen to me?"

"It doesn't matter what you say."

"Then it won't hurt to listen."

She shook her head fiercely. Now that the tears were over, she was ready to lash out again. "You never intended to stay with me, to build a life with me. It was just a temporary arrangement for you. But I can't blame you for that. You never promised, you only implied. And you never used the old candlelight-and-wine routine to romance stars into my eyes."

But the stars had been there, she thought. She'd been blinded by them. "In any case, I'm responsible for my own feelings. But I can blame you, and I can detest you, for not being honest."

"It was too complicated. I didn't know how you would react."

"I thought scientists were supposed to experiment. You are a scientist, aren't you?"

"Yes. All right. The fact is, I just didn't want to think about anything but you when I was with you." When she struggled to turn away again, he held her still. "You wanted honesty, so listen to it. Whatever I did, it was because I couldn't stop myself. I didn't want to stop myself. If that was wrong, it was because I stopped thinking with my head. If I handled it badly, it was because I didn't know how to approach you here, now. I didn't feel I could tell you about all of this. And then I was falling in love and didn't know how to deal with it. Didn't know how you would expect me to."

Frustrated, he stroked her cheek. "Sunny, I didn't think it was possible to tell you the truth. And I didn't know how…" He stopped, swore. "If it had been possible, I would have shown you more romance, but I didn't have a gift for you."

"A gift?" She'd really believed she was too weary to become annoyed again. She'd been wrong. "What the hell are you talking about?"

"Romance," he repeated, more than a little embarrassed. "Attention, flattery, the giving of gifts."

"That's the stupidest thing I've ever heard. Romance? Is that your superior species' definition of romance?" She pushed his hands away. "Idiot. Romance has nothing to do with presents or flattery. It has to do with caring and compassion, with sharing your hopes and your dreams. It means being honest."

"This is honest."

He lowered his mouth to hers. She prepared to resist, to hold him off with icy disdain. But for the first time his mouth wasn't hungry, it wasn't passionate, it wasn't desperate. It was, instead, infinitely tender. The beauty of it shimmered through her like liquid sunlight. Her defensive front of disinterest melted away like snow in the spring.

He looked at her. Was there confusion in his eyes? she wondered. It couldn't matter, she told herself. She couldn't allow herself to care so much a second time. But he laid a soothing hand on her cheek and touched his lips experimentally to hers.

He hadn't known being gentle could be so weakening. Or so fulfilling. There had always been power when he'd touched her. Bolts of power. Now there was only warmth, a quiet river of it, running through him. He wanted to share it with her, to show her how precious she was and would always be.

"I love you," he murmured. When she tried to shake her head, he only repeated the words again and again as his mouth whispered over hers.

She couldn't fight him like this. Not when the fog had rolled in over her brain and her body was sinking in some thick, syrupy darkness. Her breath shook as she tried to say his name. He covered her trembling lips with his own. Patient, so patient, as hers warmed and moved beneath his.

Time, he thought as he slowly deepened the kiss. They would take all they needed. And when the time had ended she would know that he would never love again as he had loved her.

He undressed her. Though his fingers shook from the pull of his own emotions, they didn't hurry. Button by button he loosened her shirt, pressing his lips lightly to each new opening. Softly, sweetly, he trailed his fingers over her flesh, parting the material.

There was no greed now, only an aching, bittersweet tenderness.

Surrendering, she eased his sweater up over his shoulders so that she could feel the warmth of his skin against hers. If she only had today, she would forget all the yesterdays, all the tomorrows. As his mouth met hers again, it was as though it were the first time they had kissed. The first time they had loved.

This she would remember. The heady flavor of his lips, those quiet, lovely words he spoke against her mouth. Not promises. There could be no promises. But there was the depthless green of his eyes to drown in. There was the impossible gentleness of his hands to be lost in.

He slipped her jeans over her hips, following the route with his mouth, down her thigh, over her knee and her calf. In the dim, silent room, there was no day or night. And a heart so filled with love could not break.

She enchanted him, until he believed they would always be here together, alone, with only the soft sigh of the bed shifting, yielding beneath the pressure of their bodies. Alone, with only the soothing stroke of her fingers over his skin. With only her drifting, tenuous scent swimming in his brain.

And the love he felt pulsed through his blood, seeped into his bones, until he knew he would never be free of it. There was joy in that. She would be with him, despite all distances.

He slipped into her with a yearning that was deep. She enfolded him with an unquestioning generosity. As they moved together, time stood beautifully still.

* * *

She woke, blinking in the darkness and afraid. Beside her, the bed was cool. He was gone. Panic snatched at her throat and had her rearing up. She bit back the cry and steadied herself.

He wasn't gone—or at least he hadn't gone far, for she was still on the ship, in his bed. With her heart pounding, she lay back and tried to think.

The way he had loved her had been so sweet, so kind, so patient. And so much like goodbye. She couldn't cry again, Sunny promised herself as she squeezed back tears. Crying solved nothing. If she loved him, and she did, the only thing she could do for him was to be strong.

She dressed in the dark, then went to look for him.

The ship confused her. There was another cabin, smaller than Jacob's but painted in the same pale blues. She passed through another area she assumed was the galley only because there was an empty carton of some sort of drink on a smooth, narrow counter and a metal door built into the wall that after a critical study she decided was some sort of oven.

She found him on the flight deck, sitting at the command console. His wore only his jeans. The viewing screen showed a panorama of forest and the shadow of distant ridges. He was staring through it as he spoke to the computer.

"Set coordinates for 1500 hours."

Affirmative.

"Preferred destination as close as possible to original departure data, time and position."

Understood.

"Estimate approximate flight time from lift-off to time warp."

Working... Estimate three hours, twenty-two minutes from lift-off to orbit of sun. Is closer calculation desired?

"No."

"Jacob."

He spun in his chair, swore under his breath. "Disengage."

The computer screen went blank.

"I thought you were sleeping."

"I was." Accusations, threats, pleas, sprang to her lips. She bit them back. She had promised herself she would be strong. "You're going back."

"I have to." He rose to cross to her. "Sunny, I've tried to find another way. There is none."

"But—"

"Do you love your parents?"

"Yes, of course."

"And I love mine." He took her hand, weighed it in his. "I can't begin to explain what we went through when we thought Cal was dead. My mother... She's very strong, but when the news came that he was lost, presumed dead, she was ill with grief. Days, weeks."

"I'm sorry," she said quietly. "I can only imagine how you must have felt."

He shook his head. Those days were still difficult to speak of. "And then, when we learned the truth, they both tried to accept. He was alive, and that meant everything. But to know that they would never see him again, never know." He broke off in frustration. "Maybe they can accept, especially when I explain to them that he's happy here. When I tell them about the child."

"What child?"

"Cal's—Libby's carrying a child. Didn't she tell you?"

"No." Shaken, Sunny pressed a hand to her temple. "Everything was so confused. And I... Libby's pregnant." With a little laugh, she dropped her hand. "How about that? We're going to have a niece or nephew." It seemed right, only right, that when her world was at its darkest there should be that tiny glimmer of life, and of hope, in the future.

Yet it was that same future she was losing him to.

"Having a baby only takes nine months," she began, trying to sound casual. "I don't suppose you'd consider hanging around to see whether we should buy blue or pink balloons."

It was so easy to see beyond her smile, into her eyes,

where the sadness hovered. "I can't take a chance on leaving the ship here so long—and I've already over-stayed my projected equations. Sunny, my parents have a right, a need, to know about Cal's life, about the child. Their grandchild."

"Of course."

"If I could stay… There's nothing there that means as much to me as what I've found with you. You have to believe that."

She struggled to remain calm while her world silently fell apart. "I believe that you love me."

"I do. But if I don't go back, if I don't give them that much, I could never live with myself."

She turned away, because she understood too well. "Once, when I was nine or ten, I wandered off. We were at the cabin for the summer and I wanted to explore. I thought I knew the forest so well. But I got lost. I spent a night under a tree. When Mom and Dad found me the next afternoon they were frantic. I've never seen my father cry, not like that."

"Then you know why I can't just turn my back on them."

"Yes, of course." She managed to smile as she faced him. "I'm sorry I caused such a scene before."

"Don't."

"No, really, I am. I didn't have any right to say the things I said." But, try as she might, she couldn't apologize for decking him. "I can't begin to understand what it must have been like for you all these weeks. Trying to fit in and bide your time until Cal came back."

"It wasn't so hard. I had you."

"Yes." She lifted a hand to his cheek, let it fall away. "I'm glad you did. I want you to know that."

"Sunny—"

"So when do you go?" Deliberately she moved out of reach. If he touched her, however gently, she might shatter.

"Tomorrow."

She had to lock her knees to keep them from buckling. "So soon?"

"I thought it best, for everyone."

She wondered that her smile didn't crack her face. "I'm sure you're right. But you'll want to spend a little more time with Cal. You've come a long way."

"I'll talk to him in the morning. And to Libby," he added. "I want to set things right with her."

Now the smile came more easily. "They're good for each other. You see that, don't you?"

"I'd have to be blind not to."

"Science and logic aside, sometimes emotions are the most accurate equations." Feeling stronger, she held out her hand. "I'd like to stay the night, here with you."

He brought her close, struggling not to crush her against him. "I'll come back." When she shook her head, he pulled her away. The passion was in his eyes again, and the anger. "I will. I swear it. I need a little more time, to test. I managed to work it out this far in only two years. With another two, I can make it smoother, until it's as basic as a shuttle to Mars."

"A shuttle to Mars," she repeated.

"Just trust me," he told her, drawing her back. "When I work it all out we'll have more time together."

"More time," she murmured, and shut her eyes.

Chapter 12

She left before he awakened. It seemed the best way. She hadn't slept at all. She had lain awake during the night trying to find the best way.

He had put music on, something dreamy and beautiful by a composer she hadn't heard of. Because he had yet to be born. He had adjusted the lights so that the cabin had been washed with simulated moonbeams.

To add romance. She understood that now, loved him for it. He had wanted to give her everything it was possible for him to give her on that last night. And he had given her everything but what she wanted most. A future.

It occurred to her as she thought over the twist her life had taken that up until this point all her decisions had been black-and-white. A choice was either right or wrong. But this time, this most important time, there were dozens of shades in between.

She drove back to the cabin slowly. How could she have said goodbye again? Some pains could not be endured a second time. Sunny could only hope he would understand what she was doing. She hoped she understood it.

She parked in back of the cabin and sat for a little while, studying the way the glaze of ice on the tree limbs glittered in the morning sun. Listening to the sound, the sound of almost perfect silence. Tasting the hint of coming snow in the air.

Slowly, fighting back the grief, she walked to the cabin and entered the kitchen quietly.

Libby had left a light in the window. The sight of the old kerosene lamp burning dully in the morning light brought the hateful tears to her eyes again. She swallowed them, then sat at the table to run her fingers over the wood as Jacob had only weeks before.

"You're up early."

Sunny lifted her eyes and met her sister's. "Hi." Her lips curved. "Mom."

Instinctively Libby laid a hand on her stomach. "Jacob told you. I wanted to."

"Great news is great news whatever the source." She rose to gather her sister close. There was joy here, and she clung to it. "No morning sickness?"

"No. I've never felt better."

"Cal better be spoiling you."

"Rotten." Libby drew back to brush at Sunny's fringe of bangs. Her sister's eyes were shadowed and sad. "How are you?"

"I'm okay." Because her legs felt unsteady again, she turned back to sit at the table. "I'm sorry I ran out the way I did."

"That doesn't matter." Libby was dressed in a baggy sweater and cords, her favored outfit for the mountains. Studying her, Sunny thought her sister had never been more beautiful. She wondered if she would ever carry a child, feel that love growing inside her.

"I flattened him."

"Good," Libby said, with a nod of approval. Movements automatic, she filled the teakettle with water, then set it on the burner. "Want some breakfast?"

"Later, maybe."

"Sunny, I'm so sorry."

"Don't be." Sunny reached behind her to close a hand over the one Libby had laid on her shoulder. "Really, it's all right."

"You really love him."

"Yes, I love him."

Wishing she could find a way to grant her sister the happiness she felt herself, Libby rested a cheek on Sunny's hair. "Cal says J.T.'s planning to do some more work on the equations for the time travel. To hone it down, to make it safer, and more practical, if that word can apply."

"Yes, he told me."

"He's brilliant, Sunny. Really brilliant. It's not just Cal's bragging. I read the rest of his file. And the fact that he was able to make this trip after only two years of work is proof of it. Once he finishes his testing, he'll come back."

"I hope he can." She closed her eyes. "I really hope he can." Then, with a laugh, she buried her face in her hands. "Listen to us. We're here talking about all of this as if it were the most natural thing in the world. I must still be in shock."

"After more than a year, I still wake up some mornings wondering if I imagined it all."

"But you have Cal," Sunny murmured, letting her hands fall into her lap. "He's right there to prove it's real."

"Sunny, if I—" She broke off when Cal walked into the room. She lifted her shoulders, let them fall. "Is there anything I can do?"

"No. I'm handling it, I promise you that."

"I'm going to get some fresh air," Libby announced. "Cal, take care of the tea, will you?"

A look passed between them. "Sure."

Sunny knew them both well enough to understand

that they'd planned this little bit of business so that Cal could speak to her alone.

"What do you want?" he asked when Libby had shut the door behind her. "Froot Loops or burnt toast?"

"J.T. fixed the toaster."

"Oh yeah?" He gave it a casual glance. "He's always liked to fiddle with things." The kettle began to boil, giving him another moment to think through what he wanted to say. "Sunny...I think we'll get snow before nightfall."

"Cal, why don't you relax? As tempting as it was, I didn't murder him."

"I wasn't worried about that." He poured hot water into two cups. "Not too much, anyway. It's more a matter of wanting to explain."

"That your brother's a jerk? I know that."

"He's also sensitive."

She could still be amused. That was a relief. "Are we talking about the same man? Hornblower, Jacob? Astrophysicist? The one with the bull head and the nasty temper?"

An apt description, he thought. "Yeah. I don't mean like he cries at vid—movies," he remembered. "Or that he takes it to heart when you call him names. He's sensitive where other people are concerned. Family." Not certain he was handling the situation correctly, he brought the tea to the table. "Half the time when he'd get into fights it was because someone had said some-thing about me. It used to annoy me, because I wanted to take care of it myself, but he'd always plow right in before I had the chance. And my parents...I can't think of a single time he'd forget a birthday or Mother's Day."

"They still have Mother's Day?"

"Sure."

"Cal." Absently she stirred sugar into her tea. "How did you decide to stay?"

"I didn't decide," he told her. "What I mean is, I don't think *decide* is the word. It implies choice. I couldn't leave Libby. I tried. But I've never stopped thinking about my family."

"Whether you consider you had a choice or not, it had to be difficult."

"For me it was pretty cut-and-dried. I couldn't even be sure if I'd make it back. I sent the ship and the re-ports because if there was a chance I could let them know I was alive, safe, I had to." He laid a hand over hers. "With J.T., it's different. He knows he can make it back, and if he didn't go he'd be leaving them with-out hope. He couldn't do that."

"No, he couldn't do that." She lifted her head. "It's been hard for you."

"This has been the best year of my life."

"But the adjustments, the separation..."

"If I'd been tossed back another five hundred years it wouldn't have mattered. As long as I'd found Libby."

"She's lucky to have you."

"I like to think so." He grinned, then sobered. "He loves you, Sunny."

Something flickered in her eyes before she lowered them. "Did he tell you that?"

"Yes, but he didn't have to. I saw it the first time he said your name. I guess what I wanted to tell you was that he's never felt about anyone the way he feels about you."

"Will you help me, Cal? I left before he woke up." She pressed her lips together to keep them from trembling. "I can't say goodbye."

Libby stood by the stream watching the water fight its way around the ice. In her mind she saw it as it had been in the spring, when the water had gurgled lazily over the rocks and the song of birds had been everywhere. The grass had been soft and green.

It was there that she and Cal had buried the time capsule. And there they had made love, while her heart had broken at the picture of him unearthing it again in some springtime hundreds of years ahead.

Instead, he had stayed, and it was his brother who had taken out the box they had placed there. Now it was her sister's heart that was breaking.

Whatever comfort she offered Sunny wouldn't be enough.

It seemed wrong that she should have everything while Sunny lost. She had Cal, and the home they loved, the life they were building. She had the child. With a soft smile, she pressed a hand to her stomach. The child who would come at summer's end and bind them even closer together.

Sunny would have only memories, and there was nothing Libby could do about it.

She turned her head slightly and saw Jacob.

He was only a few feet away. She hadn't heard his approach in the muffling snow. In the shadows cast by the trees she saw how much he resembled Cal. The same build, the same coloring, the same sharp facial bones. There was a measuring look in his eyes that made her wonder how long he had been standing and watching her in silence.

She didn't approach him. Though he posed no threat to her—and she admitted that she had been foolish and over-emotional ever to believe he could—he had taken her sister's heart. And broken it.

"Cal's inside." Her voice was cool and clipped. She made no attempt to be friendly.

She showed her anger differently from Sunny, he mused. Sunny exploded with hers, went straight on the attack. Apparently Libby let hers bubble and brew inside. He wondered if she realized it was just as volatile.

"I wanted to talk to you."

She had never enjoyed confrontations, but she braced for this one. "There's nothing you can say to me that would make me influence Cal to leave with you. The choice is his, whether you believe it or not. Just as it was before."

"I know." He moved slowly across the snow until he stood beside her. "It isn't something I thought I would understand or accept, but I do. Our parents will… It will mean a great deal to them when I tell them about you. About the child."

"He misses them." Her voice was thick as she battled the tide of emotion. "They should know that."

"They will."

"Why didn't you tell her?" she demanded. "How could you have let her fall in love with you when you knew you were going to leave?"

His hands fisted as he plunged them into the pockets of his pea coat. "I spent two years working, inching my way here. For one reason. Only one. To find my brother and take him home."

Her eyes smoldered at that. "You can't have him."

"No." He nearly smiled. Perhaps she was more like Sunny than he had originally thought. "And I can't have

Sunny, either. I have to live with that. She isn't the only one who fell in love. She isn't the only one to lose."

"But you knew what you were doing."

Vibrating with frustration, he faced her. For the first time she saw that his eyes were haunted and miserable. "You thought Cal would leave. Did it stop you from loving him, or him from loving you?"

"No." With a little sigh, she put a hand on his arm. "No, it didn't."

"She's strong," he said. His control had slipped a few notches when he'd heard the understanding in her voice. "She won't allow herself to hurt for long. If I can't come back…" The pain ripped through him, forcing him to take a slow, deep breath. "If I can't come back, she'll go on."

"Do you really believe that?"

"I have to." He dragged an unsteady hand through his hair. With the ache rippling through him, he told her what he hadn't been able to tell Sunny. What he hadn't wanted to face himself. "I haven't perfected the procedure. This time I was months off. The next time, if there is one, I may be years off. She may have started a new life. I have to accept that."

She smiled at him. "I study people. When you make it a profession, you learn more than tradition and social mores. You learn that real love, lasting love, is very rare. It should never be simply accepted, J.T. It should be cherished."

He gazed across the white world he was just beginning to understand. "I'll think of her every day for the rest of my life."

"Have you never heard the word *compromise?*"

"I'm not very good at it. If I could find one, I'd learn to be good at it. I can only tell you that everything I do from the moment I get back will be geared toward finding a way to return here, within a day, within an hour, of the time I left."

Moved, she leaned up and kissed his cheek. It surprised her when his arms came around her, held her. Without hesitating, she returned the embrace.

"Take care of them. Both of them."

"I will." She tightened her hold briefly, then smiled when she saw Cal walking toward them. Kissing Jacob again, she released him before she held out a hand for Cal's. "Why don't I go make some breakfast?"

"Thanks." Cal's fingers squeezed hers. "I love you."

With a quick smile, she headed back to the cabin.

"Is Sunny inside?"

Cal turned back to his brother. "She came back early." He put a hand on Jacob's arm to restrain him. "J.T., she asked me to tell you that she wishes you a safe trip but she can't say goodbye again."

"The hell with that."

"Jacob." Cal shifted to block his brother's path. "She needs to do it this way. Believe me, it won't help her if you try to see her again."

"Just cut it off clean?" Jacob pulled out of Cal's hold. "As simple as that?"

"I didn't say it was simple. There's no one who knows better how you feel than I do. If you love her," he continued, "let her have her way in this."

Holding up his hands, Jacob whirled and strode a few paces off. Pain roiled inside him, pain edged with resentment. She wouldn't even see him one last time. Already she was just a memory. Perhaps it was best, he told himself, best that he could believe she was already getting on with her life.

If he could do nothing else for her, he could honor this last request.

"All right. Tell her…" He trailed off, swearing. He would never be able to find the words for what he was feeling. Even if he'd had Cal's knack for poetry, the phrases would have fallen short.

"She knows," Cal told him. "Come on inside."

In the afternoon they drove him to the ship. He wondered if Sunny was watching from a window as they disappeared into the forest. But when he looked back, searching, the sun was glaring on the glass and he could see nothing.

Cal talked constantly, trying to fill the void with chatter. Jacob saw that he reached for Libby's hand, held it tight.

And he was denied even that, he thought. Even one last touch.

Cursing Sunny, he climbed out of the car. "I'll tell Mom and Dad everything."

Cal nodded. "Get back to the lab. I want to know that you'll come back and bring them for a visit."

"I'll be back." He embraced his brother.

"I love you, J.T."

Letting out a long breath, he broke away to turn to Libby. "Tell your sister I'm going to find a way."

"I'm counting on it." Libby blinked back tears as she handed him an envelope. "She asked me to give this to you, but to make you promise you won't open it until you get back to your own time."

He reached out, but she pulled it back. "Your word. Cal tells me you take promises seriously."

"I won't open it until I'm gone." He folded it carefully before slipping it in his pocket. He kissed her, one cheek, the other, then her mouth. "Keep well, sister."

The first tear overflowed. "And you." She turned her face into Cal's shoulder as Jacob stepped through the hatch.

"He'll be back, Libby." He lifted a hand in farewell,

then let it fall. Smiling, he pressed a kiss to her hair as she wept. "It's only a matter of time."

Inside, Jacob cleared his mind and went to work. The procedure for lift-off was basic, but he went through the routine as meticulously as a first-year pilot. He didn't want to think. Couldn't afford to.

He had known it would hurt, but he had never imagined this kind of dull, gnawing pain. It made his fingers stiff on the switches.

The lights hummed as he set the controls for ignition. Through the viewscreen he saw that Cal had moved Libby back out of harm's way. For the last time he searched the forest for signs of Sunny. There was nothing. He threw the last switch.

The ship rose gently, almost silently. He knew he couldn't afford to linger, but he kept the speed down until his brother was only a speck in the sea of white and green. With an oath, he jammed the throttle and shot through the atmosphere.

Space was soothing, the dark silence of it. He didn't want to be soothed. It would be best if he held on to his anger, his frustration. His jaw set, he engaged his computer.

"Implement coordinates to sun."

Coordinates implemented.

Seen through the viewscreen, the world was only a pretty colored ball.

Mechanically he navigated, compensating for a small shower of meteors. It was very simple, really, he thought. Now there was no traffic, commercial or private. No route patrol ships to communicate with. No checkpoints.

He hit the switch and bulleted into hyperspace. As before, his eyes narrowed, his muscles tensed, as he hurtled toward the sun. He watched dispassionately as the gauges registered the increase in outside temperature. With the viewscreen lowered, he flew blind, expertly but without the passion that had fueled him on his last voyage.

Working with the computer, he increased the speed, adjusted the angle. Meticulous and mechanical, his fingers moved over the command console. Though he was prepared, the Gs slammed him back in his chair. Holding course, he swore, filling the cockpit with his anger and his hopelessness.

Now, though his heart was thousands of miles below, there was no turning back.

Like a bullet from a gun, he shot through space and time and away from his heart.

He was breathless when the procedure was complete. A line of sweat rolled down his back. A glance at his gauges told him he had been successful.

Successful, he thought miserably, rubbing his hands over his eyes. Raising the viewscreen, he looked out on his own time.

It looked so similar, the stars, the planets, the inky darkness. There were more satellites, and in the distance he saw a blip of light he knew was a research lab. In less than thirty minutes he would join the traffic patterns. He would no longer be alone. Leaning back, he closed his eyes in quiet desperation.

She was gone.

Fate had brought him to her, then had torn him away. Fate, he thought, and his own intellect. He would use that intellect. If it took a lifetime, he would find a way to bring their lives together again.

Perhaps he would suffer over the months or years it took him to complete the necessary tests that would take him back, safely, close to the time of his lift-off. But he would get back, and he would calculate so minutely that she would barely realize he'd ever been gone.

Slowly he took the letter out of his pocket. It was all he had left of her. Some message, he thought. A few words of love and remembrance. It wouldn't be enough, he thought furiously, and ripped it open.

There was only one word.

Surprise.

Baffled, he stared at it.

Surprise? he thought. Just surprise. What kind of

last message was that? So damn typical of her, he decided, balling the paper up in his fist. Then, relenting, willing to settle for even as little as this, he smoothed it out again.

At a faint sound, he whirled in the chair.

She was standing at the doorway to the flight deck. She was deathly pale, and her eyes were glassy. But as he watched, dumbfounded, her lips moved into a smile.

"So, you got my message."

"Sunny?" He whispered her name at first, wondering if he was hallucinating. It was only one of the potential side effects of time travel. He would have to remember to make a note of it.

But he could not only see her, hear her, he could smell her. He catapulted out of the chair to grab her close, to devour her mouth like a starving man.

Then it struck him. Terrified him.

"What are you doing here?" he demanded, shaking her. "What the hell have you done?"

"What had to be done." When she swayed, he cursed her again.

"Yell at me later," she said calmly. "I think I'm going to pass out."

"No, you're not." Though he was infuriated, he lifted her as though she were fragile glass and carried her to a chair. Then he was all business.

"You're light-headed?"

"Yes." She put her hand on her temple. "It was a hell of a trip."

"Nauseous?"

"Some."

He pressed a round black button, and a small compartment opened. He pulled out a square box. From it he took a tiny, paper-thin pill. "Let this dissolve on your tongue. Idiot," he said, even as she obeyed. "You aren't prepped for traveling at warp speed."

The relief was instant. She took a long breath, pleased that she wasn't going to disgrace herself. Ignoring him for the moment, she turned to the viewscreen. The galaxy was spread out before her.

"Oh, my God." The color that had come back into her cheeks fled again. "It's incredible. Is that—is that Earth?"

"Yes." His palms were damp. If his stomach didn't settle, he'd have to resort to a pill himself. "Sunny, do you have any idea what you've done?"

"How fast are we going?"

"Damn it, Sunny."

"Yes, I know what I've done." She swiveled in the chair to rest her hands on his knees. Her eyes, when they met his, were dark and clear. "I've passed through time with you, Jacob."

"You have to be out of your mind." He wanted to shake her until her bones rattled. He wanted to hold her against him until they melted. "How could you have pulled off a ridiculous stunt like this?"

"Cal and Libby helped me."

"They helped you? They knew you'd planned this?"

"Yes." When she felt her hands begin to tremble, she sat back and folded them in her lap. She didn't want him to know how frightened she was. "I decided last night."

"You decided," he repeated.

"That's right." Her chin lifted, and she gave him a long, level look. "I talked to Cal this morning, told him what I wanted to do." Calmer now, she turned to the viewscreen again. There were lights in the sky. Stars. Instead of looking up at them, she looked out. As incredible as it was, she was hurtling through space with the only man she had ever loved. Would ever love.

Someone had to be sensible. Someone had to be calm. But he wasn't sure it could be him. "Sunny, I don't think you understand what you've done."

"I understand perfectly." She looked back at him. Yes, she was calm again, she realized. Calm, with her mind clear and her heart content. "Cal made a token protest—more for Libby's sake than mine, really. But when I spoke with her she understood. She brought me to the ship herself this afternoon, when you were busy with Cal."

"Your parents…"

"Would want me to be happy." There was a pang, a

deep one, when she thought of them. "Libby and Cal will explain everything to them." Because she was sure her legs were steady again, she rose to walk around the flight deck. "I'm not saying they won't be sad, or that they won't miss me if it isn't possible to go back. But I think my father—particularly my father—will get a tremendous charge when he thinks of where I am." She laughed. "*When* I am."

She turned back, still smiling. "Neither of us is good at compromising, J.T. With us, it's all or nothing. That's why we'll get along so well."

"I would have come back." He covered his face with his hands, then dragged them back through his hair. "Damn it, Sunny, I told you I'd come back. A year, maybe two or three."

"I didn't want to wait that long."

"You idiot, if I had managed to perfect it I'd have been back five minutes after I'd left, in your time."

Her time. It struck him so hard, so deep, that he wasn't sure he could speak. "You had no right to make a decision like this without discussing it with me."

"It's my decision." Riled, she stalked back to him. "If you don't want me, then I'll just find some nice, appreciative companions. Maybe on Mars. I can take care of myself, pal. Just consider that I've hitched a ride."

"It has nothing to do with what I want. It's what's best for you."

"I know what's best for me." She rapped a fist on his chest. "I thought it was you, but I've made one or two mistakes before." She spun away and took two steps before he grabbed her.

"Where are you going to go?" he demanded. "There's still a few thousand kilometers before we hit breathable atmosphere."

"It's a big ship."

"Sit down."

"I don't—"

"I said sit down." He gave her a none-too-gentle shove that sent her sprawling into the chair. "And shut up. I have something to say to you." When she braced her hands on the arms of the chair, he lifted a fist. "If you get up, I swear I'm going to belt you."

Seething, she sat back. "That's one term that appears to have survived the centuries."

"If I'd known what you were planning I'd have used that term before. There were risks involved here that you have no conception of. If I'd made a mistake, a miscalculation, even the slightest—"

"But you didn't."

"That's not the point."

"What is the point, Hornblower?"

"You shouldn't have done this."

She let out an impatient breath. "Well, it's no use belaboring that point, because I have done it. Why don't we move on to the next step?"

He found he had to sit himself. "You may never be able to get back."

"I know. I've accepted that."

"If you change your mind—"

"Jacob." Sighing, she rose, only to kneel beside him. "I can't change my mind unless I change my heart. And that's just not possible."

He reached out to touch her hair. "I wouldn't have asked this of you."

"I know. And if I had asked to come with you you would have given me half a dozen very logical reasons why I couldn't." She turned her face into his palm. "And you'd have been wrong. What I couldn't do is live without you."

"Sunny."

"Look at it this way. I've always felt that I was ahead of my time, kind of placed in the wrong era. Maybe I'll do better in yours."

"This was a stupid thing to do." Then he pulled her up into his lap. "Thank God you did it."

"Then you're not mad?"

He showed her just how mad he was when his mouth took hers. "When you wouldn't see me today, it was as if you'd cut out my heart. It didn't matter, because I'd wanted to leave it with you."

Tears rushed to her eyes, but she forced them back. She wanted only to smile at him. "That's almost poetic."

"Don't get used to it." Still holding her, he leaned forward to make some adjustments on the control panel.

"Can you teach me how to drive this?"

He slanted her a look. She was here, really here. And his. Forever. "I'm already terrified of the idea of you at the controls of a cruise rider."

"I'm a quick study."

"That's what I'm afraid of." He drew her back until she was settled in the curve of his arm. "I'm not sure even my world's ready for you."

"But you are."

He kissed her again, gently. "I've been ready all my life."

With a sigh, she teased his mouth until the passion simmered. "I don't suppose we could put this thing on automatic pilot or whatever."

"Not at this point."

"We did make it back, didn't we?"

He inclined his head toward the screen. "We've got a little way to go yet."

"No, I mean *back*. What year is it?"

He gestured toward the dials. "2254."

The enormity of it made her giddy. His arms made her trust. "So that makes me…287 years old." She cocked a brow. "How do you feel about older women?"

"I'm crazy about them."

"Remember that when I hit three hundred and things start to sag." She kissed him lightly. "I plan to frustrate you, annoy you and generally make your life chaos for a long time."

"I'm counting on it."

Together they watched the blue-green sphere that was home draw closer.

Epilogue

The sound of crashing waves seemed to fill the room. The clear wall opened the suite to the passion of the lightning-split sky and the boiling sea. The scent of jasmine, rich and sultry, rose on the air. Low, pulsing music echoed over the roar of waves and the violent boom of thunder.

"I was right," Sunny murmured.

Jacob shifted on the cloud bed to draw her closer. "About what—this time?"

"The storm." Her body still vibrated from passion just released. "I knew it wasn't a night for moonlight or tropical sunsets."

She had been right. But he hated to admit it. "The atmosphere didn't make that much difference."

She rolled, all but floated, to lie across him. "Is that

why you brought me here? To the place you once described to me?"

"I brought you here for a few days of relaxation."

"So that's what you brought me here for. When are
we going to relax?" She grinned before she bent down
to press kisses on his chest. "See, you're already tens-
ing up again."

He skimmed a hand over her hair. "How long have
we been married?"

Lazily she touched a button on the side of the bed.
The time flashed, the numbers suspended in the air,
then blinked off. "Five hours and twenty minutes."

"I figure we'll relax in about fifty years." His hand
wandered to her bare shoulder. "Do you like it?"

"Being married?"

"That, too. But I mean this place."

He was so sweet, she thought, the way he didn't want
her to think he was too sentimental. "I love it, and since
we're newlyweds and allowed to be mushy I'll tell you
that bringing me here was the most romantic thing
you've ever done."

"I thought you might prefer Paris, or the Intimacy
Resort on Mars."

"We can always go to Mars," she said, and giggled.
"I'm almost getting used to saying things like that. I
told you I was a quick study."

"You've been here six months."

"You are a tough nut." She slid down him to rest her cheek on his chest. "Six months," she repeated. "It took you long enough to marry me."

"I'd have had it over with in six minutes if you and my father hadn't gotten together."

"Over with?" She raised her head, her eyes dangerous. "Income tax reports are things you want to get over with."

"Income tax reports?" he repeated, blankly.

"I forgot. Unpleasant tasks," she said. "That's what you want to get over with. If marrying me was so unpleasant, why did you bother?"

"Because you would have nagged me." He winced when she pinched him. "Because I thought it was the least I could do." This time he laughed, rolling onto her as she dug her nails into his arms. "Because you're gorgeous."

"Not good enough."

"And marginally intelligent."

"Keep trying."

"Because loving you has scrambled my circuits."

"I guess that'll do." Happy, she linked her arms around his neck. "Maybe it was a lot of fuss and bother, but it was a beautiful wedding. I'm glad your father talked us into something traditional."

"It was all right, as ceremonies go." And when he'd

seen her start down the aisle on his father's arm, draped in shimmering white, he'd been struck dumb.

"I like your parents. They've made me feel very much at home." With her tongue in her cheek, she looked at him again. "Especially when they let me in on deep, dark family secrets."

"Such as?"

"The *T* in J.T." When he grimaced, she really began to enjoy herself. "It seems you were so rotten, so undisciplined, so…"

"I was just a curious child."

"…so hardheaded," she continued, without missing a beat, "that your father used to say Trouble was your middle name. And the *T* stuck. Aptly."

"You haven't seen trouble yet."

She slid up again to nip his lip. "I'm hoping I will."

After a quick kiss, he slid out of bed.

The silky sheets pooled at her waist as she sat up. "Where do you think you're going? I haven't finished with you yet."

"I forgot something." He hadn't forgotten at all. He'd been waiting for the right moment. He adjusted the lights so that they flickered like the flames of a dozen candles. Moments later, he returned with a box. "It's a gift."

"Why?"

"Because I've never given you one." He set it in her hands. "Are you going to open it or just stare at it?"

"I was enjoying the moment." With her tongue caught between her teeth, she opened the box. Inside was a teapot, squat, of cheap china, with a bird on the lid and huge, ugly daisies painted on the bowl. "Oh, God."

"I wanted you to have something from your time." He felt a little foolish, not ready to admit that he had spent months scouring antique shops. "When I saw this, it was…well, like fate. Don't cry."

"I have to." She sniffled, then raised her drenched eyes to his. "It survived. All this time."

"The best things do."

"Jacob." She made a helpless gesture, then hugged the pot. "There's nothing you could have given me that would have meant more."

"There's something else." He sat beside her. After taking the teapot, he set it aside. "Would you like to see your family for Christmas?"

For a moment, she couldn't speak. "Are you sure?"

"I'm nearly there, Sunbeam." He brushed away a tear, let it shimmer on his fingertip. "Just trust me a little while longer."

Fighting tears, she put her arms around him. "Take all the time you need. We've got forever."

* * * * *

The World of
MILLS & BOON®

HISTORICAL

*Awaken the romance
of the past*
6 new stories every month

*The ultimate in romantic
medical drama*
6 new stories every month

MODERN™

*Power, passion and
irresistible temptation*
8 new stories every month

By Request

*Relive the romance with the
best of the best*
12 stories every month

WORLD_ M&B2b